$2.00

"I want an **\[...\]** demanded.

"An apology? For what?"

"For trying to seduce me!"

There, it was out. But Sean's reaction was not at all what she had anticipated.

"For *seducing* you?" he echoed. "Oh, no, my darling Leah, I don't apologize for anything that felt so right, so necessary. As a matter of fact, I would very much like to try it again some time."

She glared at him furiously. "It'll be a cold day in hell before I let you touch me again!"

"Is that a fact?" he drawled lazily. "Well, in that case I'd better make sure that I have a very cold shower instead of the hot one I had planned on. Are you sure I can't persuade you to join me?"

KATE WALKER was born in Nottinghamshire, England, but as she grew up in Yorkshire, she has always felt that her roots were there. She met her husband at university and she originally worked as a children's librarian but after the birth of her son she returned to her old childhood love of writing. When she's not working, she divides her time between her family, their four cats and her interests of embroidery, antiques, film and theatre and, of course, reading.

Books by Kate Walker

HARLEQUIN PRESENTS®
2035—THE GROOM'S REVENGE
2082—CONSTANTINE'S REVENGE
2131—SATURDAY'S BRIDE

Harlequin Reader Service
U.S.: 3010 Walden Ave., P.O. Box 1325, Buffalo, NY 14269
Canadian: P.O. Box 609, Fort Erie, Ont. L2A 5X3

Kate Walker

FIANCÉE BY MISTAKE

TORONTO • NEW YORK • LONDON
AMSTERDAM • PARIS • SYDNEY • HAMBURG
STOCKHOLM • ATHENS • TOKYO • MILAN • MADRID
PRAGUE • WARSAW • BUDAPEST • AUCKLAND

ISBN 0-373-12150-4

FIANCÉE BY MISTAKE

First North American Publication 2000.

Copyright © 1998 by Kate Walker.

This edition published by arrangement with Harlequin Books S.A.

Visit us at www.eHarlequin.com

Printed in U.S.A.

CHAPTER ONE

SEAN GALLAGHER saw the car as soon as he rounded the corner into the quiet country lane. Saw it and recognised it as the one he had been looking for, fruitlessly, for the past couple of hours. A silver Renault, Pete had said, and here it was, right in front of him, just when he'd been about to give up.

'Got you!' he muttered, his voice rich with dark triumph. Little Miss Annie Elliot hadn't escaped from him after all.

But the next moment his mood changed abruptly. As the wind stilled for a second, revealing what the swirling eddies of snow had hidden from him until now, he jammed on his brakes with a speed and force that were positively dangerous in the treacherous conditions.

'Hell and damnation!'

Forcing his attention back to his driving, he controlled the powerful car with an effort, bringing it safely to the side of the road. The last thing he wanted was to join his quarry in the ditch.

It looked as if she had hit a patch of ice and skidded off the road. Hardly surprising, really, when you considered how the narrow lane twisted and turned, and how the snowstorm that had suddenly sprung up out of nowhere had rapidly developed into the worst blizzard in living memory.

Probably driving too fast in her eagerness to put plenty of space between herself and the mess she had left behind her, he decided cynically, getting out of the car and turning up his coat collar against the biting force of the wind. Her mind wouldn't have been on what she was doing, but full of the new lover she had abandoned Pete for.

Well, her bad luck was very definitely his gain. Or,

rather, Pete's. Personally, he didn't give a damn whether he found this woman or not. But a promise was a promise.

It was then that the silence, the total lack of movement inside the other car struck home to him, making him curse again, more violently this time. A promise was a promise, but this was a situation that neither he nor his brother had anticipated. What if the woman in the driving seat was badly injured, or worse?

With his head bent, his hair blown into wild disarray, he made his way towards the Renault as swiftly as he could, with his feet slipping and sliding over the frozen surface of the road.

'Can I help you?'

They had to be the most wonderful words in the world, Leah thought hazily. The trouble was that with her mind still spinning from the panic of only moments before she couldn't quite believe she had actually heard them.

Was it possible that they were not real, but only a figment of her imagination?

'Can you…?'

As she echoed the question she didn't dare to open her eyes, fearful that if she did she would discover that her deep-voiced rescuer didn't exist.

'Do you need help? Are you all right?'

The man's tone—for it was unquestionably a masculine voice, dark and huskily sensual—sharpened noticeably on the question.

'Are you hurt?'

'Don't think so.'

Mentally Leah checked herself over, carefully ticking off parts of her body on an invisible list.

Legs, two, intact. Arms, ditto, though one felt rather sore, as if badly bruised. Her shoulders ached miserably, and she felt as if she had jarred her back in the frantic effort to control the dangerous spin of the car, but it seemed she was still in one piece.

Unless…

Her closed lids flew open, violet eyes focusing swiftly on her own reflection in the car's mirror.

No. Relief set in as she realised that the damp trail down her left cheek was not, as she had feared, the trickle of blood. Instead it had been caused by a single weak tear, probably the result of shock and disorientation. She hadn't even been aware of having shed it.

Suddenly she was desperately, horribly cold. She was unable to decide whether the shiver that shook her was the result of delayed reaction to the danger she had been in or something else. Equally, it might have been a purely physical response to the icy wind that sneaked past the powerful frame of the man who held the car's front door wide open.

'Could you give me a definite answer?'

The voice was harsh now, jolting her out of her near dreamlike state and back into full awareness of the present. Of course, he must have seen her crash—seen her small car skid suddenly, veering right off the road and onto the rough verge at its edge. Naturally he was concerned.

'I'm sorry…'

The words died in her throat, shrivelled into an unbelieving silence as she shifted in her seat, her eyes finally focusing on the rearview mirror. With her own head no longer blocking the view from the door, she caught her first glimpse of her rescuer, and couldn't believe what she saw.

'I…'

Dear God, perhaps she was hallucinating after all. It must be the after-effects of shock, or perhaps she had hit her head hard enough to scramble her wits. Knights on white chargers didn't exist in reality, and they certainly did not appear in such a devastating physical form. She couldn't be seeing what she thought was there.

'Of course I can.' This time she managed to get the words out, swivelling in her seat to face him as she spoke. 'I—I'm fine.' Oh, Lord, this was no better! In fact it was far worse. No matter how hard she forced herself to concentrate, her fuddled brain still registered exactly the same

thing, confirming that what she had seen in the mirror was
not the illusion she had believed, but actual fact.

The mirror image had softened the impact of hard,
strongly carved cheekbones, a straight nose, a firm slash of
a mouth, stunningly bright blue eyes and a shock of long-
ish, rather wild black hair. The dramatic effect of that forceful profile etched against the darkness was matched by the
imposing height and strength of the body that filled the
open doorway, the man before her having to stoop quite
considerably in order to look her in the eye.

But the impossible thing was that those features, that
powerful frame, could only belong to one man. And it was
his identity that made Leah doubt her sanity at this moment.

'No!'

Weakly she shook her head, hoping to dispel the tormenting vision. Even in her wildest dreams she had never
fantasised that she might meet up with Sean Gallagher.
After all, he was the latest TV heart-throb, the man whose
appearance in a hugely successful drama series had had the
effect of bringing almost the entire female population of
Great Britain to a complete halt every Thursday night.

'No?' her rescuer questioned, no softening evident in his
tone. 'Is that, No, there's nothing wrong, or, No, you're not
fine after all? For God's sake, woman! Can you string two
coherent words together or not?'

'Of course I can!'

Incensed by his rudeness, Leah's impatience matched his
now, anger sharpening her words. So much for fantasy, she
told herself ruefully. Sean Gallagher might be the hunk of
the year—of the decade—but it seemed that his stunning
looks were in no way matched by an equally appealing
character.

'Yes, I'm fine. No, I'm not injured—at least as far as I
can tell. But as I haven't tried to stand up yet I can't exactly
swear to the total accuracy of that statement. Does that
satisfy you, or would you like to interrogate me a bit
more?'

'Well, on the evidence of that outburst, I would have to

agree that you are obviously *not* badly hurt.' The thread of dry humour that warmed his attractive voice had an effect that was almost as devastating as the smile that softened and curved his hard mouth. 'But I take exception to your use of the word "interrogate"—'

'Except away!' Leah returned sharply, riled by the mockery in his words. 'You may be God's gift to women, but you're clearly not going to win any prizes for sensitivity. Has no one ever told you that someone who has just hit a patch of black ice and spun off the road into a ditch might actually be some way from fully in control? There is such a thing as shock, you know, and...'

'I know, and I'm sorry.'

Unexpected gentleness drew the force of her tirade, reducing her to stunned silence. He actually looked shame-faced too, she acknowledged, grudgingly conceding him a favourable point or two.

'I was pretty shocked myself. After all, I've driven along this road day and night for weeks without seeing anyone. So you can imagine how I felt when I came round the corner to find your car nose-down in the ditch. Was that what happened? You hit a patch of ice?'

'I think so.'

Leah's voice was no longer as confident as it had been before. Her memories of the actual accident were hazy, and trying to recall them was distinctly unsettling.

'I was driving along—crawling, really, because of the weather—and suddenly the car seemed to have a will of its own. It went into an uncontrollable skid, and the next thing I knew was that I was here...'

And where *was* here? She should have been over halfway to her mother's by now, but in the appalling driving conditions she had missed the exit off the motorway and had had to take a smaller side road in order to get back to the route she wanted.

She'd made another wrong turning later, and was then hopelessly lost. As a result, she wasn't at all sure where she'd ended up, only that it was somewhere in the wilds of

Yorkshire, and obviously miles from anywhere. She couldn't remember when she'd last seen a single house, let alone anything resembling civilisation.

And, if she was honest, her thoughts hadn't exactly been on what she was doing. Foolishly, considering the whirling snow and swiftly dropping temperature, she had been distracted by the problems that had been fretting at her mind all week. That was why she had missed her turn-off in the first place.

'I think you'd better get out of there. It doesn't look exactly safe,' her rescuer advised. '*Can* you stand?'

'I think so.'

It was more of a struggle than she had anticipated. For one thing the front of the car was at a very awkward angle, one that necessitated an ungainly shuffle and an even less ladylike scramble in order to get her legs out of the door.

'Here—' Sean Gallagher held out a hand encased in a dark leather glove. 'Let me help.'

It was only a hand, Leah told herself. And all he wanted to do was *help*. So why was she suddenly gripped by a rush of something that was neither fear nor excitement but a disturbingly volatile mixture of the two? Why did she feel that to touch him would...?

Would what? Now you're being silly, she reproved herself sharply. Did she expect that just to take hold of his hand would spark off some explosion? Contaminate her in some way? Be sensible, Leah!

But common sense and reason seemed to have nothing to do with the way she was feeling. It was as if some primitive instinct older than time was warning her not to risk even the slightest contact with this man.

'I can manage!'

She heard the words before she actually realised that her tongue had formed them and knew they were a mistake from the way his dark head went back, the long, powerful body stiffening in hostile response to her tone.

'Suit yourself.'

It was curt, sharply dismissive, but what else had she

expected? After all, her own inner unease had tightened her throat, making her declaration sound uncharacteristically tart and cold.

And, to compound the problem, her undignified scramble to get out of the car without any help had taken more effort than she'd realised. It had also resulted in the rucking up of the skirt of her red velvet dress, pulling it high up on her thighs.

Not for the first time Leah cursed the way her sudden decision to spend an extra day of the Christmas holidays at home had meant leaving in a rush straight after the agency's party.

Her mother wasn't even expecting her, believing that she wouldn't be setting out until tomorrow morning. But Paula Elliot had sounded so sad and lonely when Leah had phoned her that she had decided on impulse to leave earlier. After all, Christmas was a time for families, and, without her father there, there was only Leah herself to fill that space in her mother's life.

If she had planned more carefully, she could have found time to change into something much more appropriate for the long drive north. As it was, not anticipating the blizzard conditions that had set in once she was on the motorway, she had simply pulled on a warm coat over her party wear.

But a tight velvet Lycra sheath was definitely *not* the easiest of garments in which to manoeuvre her way out of a car perched at such a difficult angle. Particularly not with six feet two of very masculine hunk watching her every move with blatantly appraising interest.

'Very nice,' he murmured as Leah inched her way forward, wanting desperately to be upright and decently covered again as quickly as possible.

Those amazing blue eyes were on the slender length of her legs, brightening noticeably as an unwary movement pushed the tight skirt even higher, revealing the pale flesh of her thighs above the lacy tops of her stockings.

'So tell me, what do you do for an encore?' he asked provocatively.

'Nothing!'

Leah aimed for freezing distance and missed it by a mile. Her snapped retort ended with a gasp of shock as, with her feet finally on the ground, she realised just how icy the road had become. The worn leather soles of the old shoes she wore for driving had no grip at all on the treacherous surface, and she felt her feet begin to slide from under her.

With a cry of panic, her hand went out automatically to grab at the nearest thing for support.

The 'nearest thing' was Sean Gallagher's arm. Leah's flailing fingers closed over the soft wool of his jacket sleeve just as, reacting with swift reflexes, he moved his other hand to come round her waist. He took the full weight of her body on that one arm with as much ease as if she had been a petite slip of a thing, and not five feet ten in her stockinged feet and built on decidedly generous lines, with curving hips and softly voluptuous breasts.

'There will be *no* encore, Mr Gallagher!' Leah managed, rather breathlessly.

'Pity,' he drawled. 'I was enjoying the show.'

He didn't react to her use of his name. Probably he was well used to having people, especially women, recognise him immediately. It would be one of the burdens of fame.

Or, more likely, this man would consider it one of the perks of his job. Certainly he had appeared in the gossip columns as frequently as he had on the television, and with an ever-changing cast of beautiful women in the role of his partner.

Though just lately she hadn't read very much about him, Leah recalled. Probably because he had been busy filming the latest series of *Inspector Callender*. She doubted very much that his social life could have ground to any sort of halt.

'You put on a great performance.'

Leah could hear the smile in Sean's voice even though she couldn't see his face. She was pressed against his chest, held too close to be able to look up at him.

'"Performance"!' she spluttered, struggling to twist free

from the strength of his hold. 'It was no such thing! If you think—'

But movement was a mistake. Instead of loosening his grip, he tightened it painfully, crushing her even closer to the warmth of his body. She was so near to him that she could feel the steady beating of his heart under her cheek.

'Calm down.' His voice was softer now, warm as the touch of his hand on her face, stilling her instantly. 'You've had a shock. Take a minute or so to recover. Breathe slowly, deeply.'

Soothed by the gentle stroke of his thumb over her cheek, Leah obeyed automatically. But if breathing deeply was meant to calm her, it had exactly the opposite effect. It only added to her awareness of him in a new and disturbing way. The scent of some clean, tangy cologne tantalised her nostrils, but mixed in with it was the subtle, uniquely personal scent that was his alone.

Leah suddenly felt as if something had short-circuited inside her brain. She couldn't think clearly, couldn't focus on anything other than the warmth and strength that enclosed her, the pressure of Sean's body all along the length of her own.

Her heart seemed to be racing in double time, sending her blood pounding through her veins until her head swam. There was a hot, tight knot of excitement deep inside her that, contrarily, made her shiver convulsively.

'Are you cold?'

Being so very close, Sean couldn't have missed her reaction. His hands closed over her arms, sliding under her coat, smoothing the soft skin below the short sleeves of her dress.

'You're frozen!' Concern sounded in his voice and he increased the pressure of his touch. 'You need to get your blood moving...'

How could that be? Leah wondered dazedly. How could her skin be cold when inside she felt so burning hot? And her blood didn't need any assistance. Already it was searing through her with the white-hot force of molten lava.

There was one thing she did need, though, and the force of that desire was so great that she just couldn't fight it.

With a low murmur of sensual awareness, she lifted her head and pressed her lips to Sean Gallagher's neck, her mouth soft against the warm strength of the taut muscle of his throat. The roughness of a day's growth of stubble abraded her cheek and the faint salt taste of his skin made her tongue tingle.

For the space of a heartbeat she felt him stiffen in shock, and knew the fear of rejection. That momentary panic was enough to bring home to her the foolishness of what she had just done, but before she had time to react the hostile tension in his long body suddenly changed to a new and very different sort of awareness. Leah had perhaps a second or two to register the change before he moved again.

'So that's your game, is it?' he muttered, swinging her round sharply, so that instead of being at his side she was now clamped firmly against him.

Her breasts were crushed against the hard wall of his chest, her pelvis tight against his. Then, as he leaned back against her car, he pulled her between his legs so that she felt enclosed by him on three sides. The bite of the wind receded as she felt the heat of his body reach her even through the layers of their clothes.

Sean's mouth came down onto hers, taking it without care or consideration, crushing her lips back against her teeth and forcing a cry of shocked response from her. If her blood had seemed hectic moments before, now she felt that it was positively incandescent.

When his tongue probed the sensitive interior of her mouth she moaned out loud, as if the action had been a more intimate invasion. She couldn't control her instinctive response to the arrow of need that sliced through her, making her writhe in an uncontrolled movement that drew a low growl from deep in Sean's throat. It seemed as if some wild, electric charge had passed through every inch of her body, setting it alight with burning, tingling excitement.

She had no awareness of the darkness around them. She

didn't feel the stinging sensation of the whirling snow as it fell against her face, nor the icy drifts that pooled around her feet in the well-worn shoes. There was only herself and this man and the blazing electrical storm they had lit between them. Leah whimpered in blind delight as rough hands pushed under her coat, finding and closing over the sensitised swell of her breasts under the scarlet velvet.

With shocking suddenness Sean broke the intimate contact, wrenching his mouth away from hers with a violent imprecation. She was his brother's fiancée! For several seconds more he swore with savage and unnerving eloquence, pushing her away from him with such force that she slid dangerously on the treacherous road surface.

'And what was all that about?' The blazing fury in his voice could be heard even above the wild cacophony of the howling wind. 'Just what did you think you were doing?'

How could she answer that? Leah didn't dare to even look into his face, keeping her eyes fixed on the ground as she tried to impose some order on her wildly confused thoughts.

What *had* she been doing? What had possessed her to throw herself at a man she had never met in her life before? A man she knew nothing about other than the stories in the tabloids and the fact that his face and form appeared on her television set once a week?

'I—didn't think.'

'You didn't think!' he echoed scathingly. 'Oh, I can believe that! But it wasn't your mind that was driving you, was it, Miss Elliot?'

That brought Leah's head up in a rush, wide, shocked eyes going to his face. How did he know her name? Where...?

But as her gaze focused on his strongly carved features the question in her mind never got past her lips. Instead it was stopped by her own hand, her fingers coming up to cover her mouth, the shock that kept her silent turning her eyes dark as pansies.

It was only now that she realised he had kept part of his

face turned away from her. When he had opened the car door, and again when he had held out a hand to help her, she had only seen his right profile, the left staying hidden by the darkness. The rest of the time she hadn't been looking at him and—hot colour flamed in her cheeks—she had kept her eyes closed when he had kissed her.

'Sean!'

Now, for the first time, she could see all of his face, and the sight made her breath catch harshly in her throat. In spite of the darkness, there was no mistaking the devastating effect of the raw, jagged line that ran down his face from the corner of one eye, angling away from his mouth to end just on the strong, forceful jaw.

The barely healed scar was obviously recent, clearly the result of some dreadful accident. The handsome looks that had won Sean Gallagher so many fans were ruined; the face that adorned thousands of publicity photographs was destroyed for ever.

Watching her intently, Sean had seen the direction of her gaze, the response she couldn't disguise.

'Pretty, isn't it?' His cynicism was brutal.

'Oh, Sean!'

Shock and sympathy drove every other thought from her mind. Reacting purely instinctively, she moved forward impetuously, only realising as he flinched back, away from her, that she had actually lifted a hand as if to touch his damaged face.

'No way, lady!' he warned roughly. 'I don't fall for that trick twice in a row.'

'It was no *trick*!'

Furious at the way he had misinterpreted her gesture of concern, Leah actually stamped her foot hard, regretting her impulsive act instantly as it sent a spray of freezing snow over her feet and legs.

'What sort of person do you think I am?'

'The sort of *female...*' deliberately he emphasised his use of a different noun '...who throws herself at any available man without a thought for the one she's left behind.'

The arrogance of the man! He actually believed that just because he was a TV star any and every woman must be crazy about him, available solely for his pleasure! But then the exact words Sean had used hit home with a worrying clarity.

'What do you know about any men in my life?'

She just managed to get the words out before the truth exploded inside her head with a force that made her head reel.

It didn't matter how Sean Gallagher knew about Andy—if in fact he knew anything, and wasn't just making a lucky guess. What mattered was that *she* hadn't spared the other man a thought at all, not since Sean had appeared so unexpectedly.

Leah bit down hard on her bottom lip as her conscience reproached her bitterly. For the shock of the accident to have temporarily driven all thought of the man who had asked her to marry him from her head was one thing. But to discover that the man she had parted from only that evening had been completely wiped from her mind was quite another. How could she be so foolish—so shallow?

Sean's smile in response to her question was cold, dangerous.

'I get the impression that you're the sort of woman who uses her undeniable charms to entrap poor, weak fools, only to chew them up and spit them out when you're done with them.'

'And on what evidence do you base this outrageous attack on my character? You don't know—'

'I don't need to *know*.' Sean's icy response slashed through her indignant protest. 'I have eyes to see.'

A contemptuous wave of his hand and the downward flick of his eyes made Leah suddenly aware of just how she must look.

Her long dark hair had fallen from its elegant coil and now tumbled in wild disarray around her face. Her skirt seemed to have stuck high up on her thighs, still revealing the lacy stocking tops, and her coat now hung wide open, exposing the smooth white curves of her breasts above the clinging, low-cut bodice. The wind had whipped up a hectic colour in her cheeks, making her eyes unnaturally bright above them.

Unable to bear Sean's cold-eyed scrutiny, Leah pulled her flapping coat closely round herself like a defensive shield, tugging the belt tight at her waist.

'I was at a *party*, for God's sake! It is Christmas—peace and goodwill and all that!'

'Goodwill to *all* men!' he flung back at her. 'Or just a select few?'

'Now look here—' Leah began, purple eyes flashing fire.

But the full effect of her anger was ruined by the way that her teeth chattered against each other, and the fact that she was shaken by a sudden, convulsive shiver. The snow was still falling steadily, now coming down thicker than ever, and in the thin-soled shoes her feet were like blocks of ice. With a grimace of distress, she shifted uncomfortably, trying to ease them.

'Oh, for God's sake!' Sean exclaimed impatiently. 'We can't stay here like this. We'll freeze if we do.'

'I couldn't agree more.'

Leah was glad of any excuse to end this embarrassing confrontation. All she wanted was to get her car back on the road and be on her way. Sean Gallagher might have seemed to be a knight coming to the rescue of a damsel in distress, but appearances were definitely deceptive. He *appeared* to be the most devastatingly attractive man she had ever met, but his character had to be the most unpleasant of any she had encountered in all her twenty-five years.

'If you could just help me move my car...' she began, her voice failing as she saw his dark head move in obdurate denial of her request.

'No chance,' he stated flatly. 'There's no way we can do anything with it without a tow-truck and some chains, and even then I doubt if it will start. I mean, look at it.'

Following the contemptuous wave of one hand, Leah had to admit he spoke nothing but the truth. Leaning at a perilous angle, its front wheels deeply embedded in the ditch and the snow piling up heavily all around it, the Renault looked totally immovable. It would take professional know-how and equipment to enable her to continue her journey.

'Then perhaps you could drive me to the nearest garage or house.'

She looked hopefully to where Sean's car was parked at the side of the road. A heavy layer of snow had built up on its bonnet and roof while they were talking, but it looked in much better shape than her own vehicle.

'Please.' Tact made her add the last word, though she felt very far from wanting to be strictly polite.

A harsh, humourless laugh left her in no doubt as to exactly what he thought of that idea.

'The nearest garage, my dear Ms Elliot, is more than ten miles in that direction.' He gestured back towards the way he had come. 'I've just negotiated that road once on the way here, and believe me it was no fun at all in this weather. I've no intention of doing it again and risking my life for anyone. Have you tried the emergency services?'

'I'm not a member of a breakdown service or anything like that. Oh, I know!' she exclaimed as she saw the scathing look that told her exactly how he felt about *that*. 'I probably should have joined—as I'm sure *you* did—ages ago! But I only took possession of this car last weekend. And besides, I'd need a mobile phone to call them from here—something I don't run to on my salary.'

She glanced at the sleek and obviously expensive lines of his own BMW. A new light brightened her eyes and she looked at him expectantly.

'I suppose you've got the very latest model in your car. I could—'

As a matter of fact, no, I haven't,' Sean put in coolly. 'When I'm on the road I prefer to be unobtainable. And I know for a fact that there are no houses any closer than my own cottage. One of the reasons I bought it in the first place was because it is so isolated.'

'But what can I do? How am I going to get home?' A note of desperation threaded through the question.

Broad shoulders under the navy woollen jacket lifted in a dismissive shrug.

'Strikes me you've got two possible choices. You can stay here till morning…'

The look of scorn Leah turned on him made it only too plain that she wasn't going to take that suggestion seriously. She'd freeze before midnight.

'Or?'

'Or you can come with me. My house isn't far from here. We should make it before the roads become impassable if we're careful—and quick. You'll have to leave your car, I'm afraid. But as no one's likely to be able to move it, even if they were out in this blizzard, it should be safe enough. You can spend the night with me.'

'Spend the night with you!' Leah echoed in blank disbelief. 'You have got to be joking!'

At last her brain seemed to be functioning again. The idea of getting into this man's car and letting him drive her off to God knew where was not one that appealed in the slightest. She didn't trust him as far as she could throw him, and he had already proved to be extremely dangerous in more ways than one.

When her uncomfortable conscience put in the reminder that, judging by her earlier behaviour, she probably had more to fear from her own foolish impulses than anything Sean Gallagher might do, she pushed it aside furiously.

'No way! I'd rather take my chances with the elements!'

As her defiant words were whipped away on the wind she nerved herself for his response, expecting an angry protest laced with dark scorn at her foolishness.

It never came. Instead he shrugged again, even more dismissively than before.

'Your choice, lady.'

Already he was turning away.

'Have a good night.'

Leah watched, open-mouthed, in frank disbelief. He

couldn't mean it! She couldn't believe that he would actually leave her here.

But it seemed that he would. He had turned his back on her and was moving purposefully towards the dark, sleek shape of his parked car. Without even his ambiguous presence the silent lane seemed suddenly very dark and cold, and full of darkly threatening shadows.

'You can't do this!' Her words had to be pitched high against the manic howling of the wind. 'You can't just go and leave me here alone!'

For a brief second he paused, glanced back, eyes narrowed against the whirling snow.

'Try me,' he tossed at her, and turned back towards his car.

CHAPTER TWO

HE MEANT it too, Sean told himself as he strode away from her. Never once in all the thirty-four years of his life had he left a woman in a position of need when he could offer help, but there was always a first time, and this was it.

This woman was far more trouble than she was worth, and quite frankly the thought of letting her into his house, the home he had kept as his own very private haven until now, was not something that appealed in the slightest.

He couldn't work out just what it was about this particular female that affected him so badly, but it seemed as if his thinking processes, normally as cool and rational as any scientist's, had seized up from the moment he had left his car and headed for hers.

But could he really leave her here, alone and unprotected, in such appalling weather conditions?

His steps were already slowing when he heard her voice behind him.

'Wait! Please!'

She had finally pulled her skirt down, he noted automatically as he swung round in response to the sharp cry of distress. And the black coat was now fastened close across that stunning cleavage. Sean didn't know whether relief or disappointment was uppermost in his mind. He only knew that it was a damned sight easier to think more clearly when there was so much less of her body on display.

'Changed your mind? Decided to see sense?'

'I—realise I have no choice.'

The admission had had to be dragged from her, her stilted tone said. Her reluctance to speak to him was emphasised by the way she held her head proudly upright, those amazing violet eyes watching him as if he was something particularly unpleasant that a cat had just brought in.

'I'll freeze if I have to stay here. So if your offer of shelter still stands I'd—like to take you up on it.'

'Like' obviously didn't come in to it. She knew she had no alternative, and she hated being obliged to admit it.

'In that case we'd better get moving. Do you have anything you want to bring with you?'

'My case. It's in the boot.'

She was turning back to the Renault as she spoke, her keys in her hand, but Sean reached out and took them from her.

'I'll fetch it. You get in the car.'

He didn't want to be already in his car when she slid in beside him, didn't want to subject himself once more to the sight of those long, slender legs as she swung them inside and settled down in her seat. He needed to get back in control, remember what all this was about.

He took the few moments needed to open the boot and take out the small, battered suitcase in order to draw a couple of deep, calming breaths and impose some sort of order on his thoughts.

'Get a grip!' he muttered to himself furiously. 'All you have to do is to take her to the cottage and keep her there until Pete comes to collect her.' A promise was a promise after all.

But he had made that promise in complete ignorance, blind to any possible repercussions. He had been barely awake when his brother had phoned, dragged from a rare deep sleep by the shrill ringing of the telephone.

'Sean?' Pete's voice had been sharp and urgent, in contrast to his own near inarticulate growl on picking up the receiver.

Hearing it, Sean had shaken himself awake and sat up swiftly, leaning up against the arm of the settee on which he had fallen asleep.

'What's wrong?' Because something *had* to be wrong to put that note in his brother's voice.

'She's left me.' It was a stark, bleak announcement. 'Says there's someone else.'

'She? Your fiancée? But the wedding's—'

'In the New Year, right. Or, rather, correction—it *was* to have been. But Annie's called it off. She even gave me back the ring.'

Why wasn't he surprised? Sean wondered cynically. Women. There wasn't one of them who could be trusted. He knew that only too well. But he had hoped that for his kid brother things might turn out better.

'When did this happen?'

'Just now! We were having lunch at my place—our own private Christmas celebration, seeing as we won't be to-gether on the day—and it was obvious that something was wrong. When I asked her what it was, she just came right out with it. Said there was someone else, and then she left. She drove off in an almighty rush and I couldn't follow her. I'd…'

'Had rather too much to drink?' Sean finished for him as he hesitated. It was there in the slight slur of his brother's words, the emotion that he wouldn't normally have shown.

'A lot too much,' Pete admitted ruefully. 'There's no way I'm remotely fit to drive. That's why I thought of you.'

'Me?' Sean stared at the receiver as if it was actually his brother. 'What can I do?'

'You can go after her for me. No, listen, she wasn't go-ing home to Hexham but to her parents' for Christmas. And they live in Carborough.'

Which was a long way south. To get there, she would have to pass Appleton village, Sean realised, seeing the direction in which his brother's thoughts were heading.

'Pete, be sensible! What am I supposed to do? Throw myself in front of the car?'

'There won't be any need for that. You see, she always breaks her journey at this all-night café—The Night Owl. Do you know it?'

Sean managed a murmur that might have been agree-

ment. But his brother didn't seem to need any encourage-
ment.

'All you have to do is be there—say between six and
eight, to allow for any margin of error either way. When
she arrives you just hang onto her...'

'"Hang onto her"!' Sean echoed, raking one hand
through the darkness of his hair. 'Look, baby brother, what
am I supposed to do—kidnap her?'

'Oh, you'll manage something,' Pete declared airily, but
then suddenly his mood changed. 'Please, Sean.'

Sean knew there was no way he could resist the appeal
in his brother's voice. After all, he owed him plenty after
the past months. Pete had been there when he was needed.
He could hardly let him down now.

'I don't even know what she looks like. I haven't met
the woman yet, remember, and she doesn't even know I'm
your brother.'

But that could be an advantage—if he decided to go
along with Pete's crazy plan.

'You can't miss her. Tall, dark hair, blue eyes. Oh, and
she drives a silver Renault—H reg. Please, Sean, do this
for me.'

Sean sighed, knowing he had no alternative. 'Just tell me
one thing,' he said. 'Is she worth it?'

'More than you'll ever know,' his brother assured him.
'Oh, I know I can't expect an old cynic like you to believe
that, but just you wait. One day it'll hit you too. You'll
meet someone who'll knock you right off balance the way
Annie's done to me, and you'll never be the same again.'

And pigs might fly supersonic, Sean told himself privately. He had had more than enough of so-called romance
to last him several lifetimes. And, even more privately, he
doubted that his brother's fiancée would ever consider going back to him, no matter how much talking they did. But
he supposed everyone deserved a second chance.

'All right, I'll do it,' he said resignedly. 'But you'd better
get yourself sobered up pretty damn quickly, and get down
here fast.'

He would give it a couple of hours, no more, he told himself, replacing the receiver and getting to his feet. Just long enough to eat the supper he hadn't felt like preparing earlier—or lunch, either, come to that. The Night Owl had a very good reputation, so perhaps now was the time to try it out. He would eat his meal, taking his time over it, and if Annie Elliot turned up then he'd take it from there.

'Is something wrong?'

The soft question dragged Sean back to the present with a jolt. He had no idea how long he'd been standing there, his hand on the suitcase, lost in his thoughts.

'No. No problem.'

Giving himself a mental shake, he pulled out the case and slammed the boot shut, carefully locking the car after him. Not that it was likely that anyone would make off with it. It would need skilled help to get it out of the ditch, and already the snow was piling up around it.

Hell, the weather was far worse than he had anticipated. And it was getting more dangerous with every minute that passed. They'd be lucky to make it to the cottage before the road closed completely.

Which meant that Pete would have an impossible job getting down here from Hexham. Which also meant that he would be stuck with the errant fiancée for far longer than the few hours his brother had implied.

Neither thought was the sort to improve on his already bad mood as he dumped the suitcase on the back seat of his own car, slamming the door after it in an echo of his feelings.

'Have we far to go?' his passenger asked as he slid into the driver's seat and put his key into the ignition.

'Five miles or so. We'll have to crawl every inch of the way, but we should make it.'

He was concentrating on getting the car going, breathing a silent word of thanks when the engine caught first time. He didn't want to be stranded here for any longer than he absolutely had to—and for reasons that had nothing at all to do with the weather.

From the moment he had got into the car he had been supremely physically aware of the woman in the passenger seat. At least her coat was now firmly wrapped around her body. But those long legs were stretched out dangerously close to his own, and just the memory of the delicate lace at the top of the gossamer-fine black stockings was enough to dry his throat, so that he licked his lips in a betraying gesture.

'The trouble is that this looks as if it will settle.' Anxiety threaded through her words. 'Is your home very isolated?'

'You could say that. I don't have any near neighbours, that's for sure.'

Sean was grateful for the way that the whirling blizzard forced him to keep his attention on the road. One glance at the woman beside him had been enough to threaten his concentration once and for all.

Pete had said that she was a looker, but he had put that down to love being blind. He had had enough experience of the fairer sex to know that, as with many a brightly wrapped parcel, the outer appearance often totally belied the truth of the contents.

What he hadn't been prepared for was the instant pull he felt towards this woman, the overwhelming force of purely physical attraction that had tied his nerves into knots. Not that there was anything remotely *pure* about his feelings, he told himself wryly. Just the whispering sound of silk against silk as she uncrossed her legs had his lower body tightening in instant response.

'Then we could be stuck for ages—*days*.' Her voice showed how little the idea appealed to her. 'You said there was a town back the way you came. Perhaps you'd better turn around and—'

'And risk getting completely stranded in the worst snowstorm this decade? No way, lady! You might be prepared to put your life in danger that way, but quite frankly the idea doesn't appeal to me at all. I have first-hand experience of just what it feels like to be in a car that's out of control, and, believe me, it's not the sort of thing I care to repeat.'

That brought her head swinging round, her long hair flying so that it caught against his cheek, making him shiver in reaction. Her face was a pale blur in the shadows as she turned to him.

'Was that how it happened? A car crash?'

For one awful moment he thought that she was going to put a hand on his arm, and instinctively he stiffened, silently communicating his rejection of the possible gesture. But all the same his heart accelerated wildly as he stared determinedly out through the windscreen, struggling to catch glimpses of the darkened road through the whirling snow and the rhythmic movement of the wipers.

'I'm sorry.' Her voice was low and soft. 'I shouldn't have said that.'

'Why not?' Sean shrugged off her concern. 'It's a fact, after all. But I don't need your pity...'

'It wasn't *pity*! I meant, obviously you don't want to talk about it, so I shouldn't intrude. You must want to forget...'

'Forget!' It came on a harsh bark of laughter, one that was totally devoid of any trace of humour. 'If I *could* forget it would make things easier. It's remembering that's hell. If I close my eyes...'

He didn't even have to do that. It was there, in his mind, just behind his eyes. If he let his control drop it would all come rushing back.

'No!'

This time she did move to clutch at his arm, but in a gesture of panic rather than the sympathy he had dreaded earlier. All the same, the touch of her hand seemed to sear over the exposed skin of his wrist, as if her fingers had been white-hot, and he couldn't control the impulse to shake himself free.

'Oh, don't worry, sweetheart, I don't plan on doing that right now. There are those who value your pretty face too much to see it mangled by flying glass.'

His brother, for one, and he would do well to remember that. She was Pete's fiancée, for God's sake! The girl his

brother loved and wanted to marry. Which meant she was
strictly out of bounds to the likes of him.

'I didn't mean...' Her voice trembled, and out of the
corner of his eye he could see that she was shivering.

'I'm sorry, are you cold?'

Glad of the opportunity to distract himself, he moved
swiftly to turn up the heating, barely hearing her murmured
words of thanks as he kept his eyes glued to the little he
could see of the road ahead.

At least he recognised the turn-off to the driveway of his
cottage. In reality it was little more than a track, easy
enough to miss at the best of times.

'Almost there.' He hoped he sounded more reassuring
than he actually felt. 'Though this bit might be tricky. This
road's bad enough even in decent weather. I doubt if I'll
be able to dodge the pot-holes now that they're under six
inches of snow, so you'd better hang onto your seat.'

He cursed himself for opening his mouth when, taking
his instruction literally, she did just as she was told. The
movement of her hands to fasten over the sides of her seat
meant that her coat fell away from her body once more,
and that, together with the heat in the car, wafted a heady
perfume straight towards him.

The scent was like the woman herself. Superficially rich
and floral, it deepened to a stronger, muskier undertone that
made him want to groan aloud with the force of the memories it brought to his mind. It was impossible not to recall
how she had cuddled close to him, the soft warmth of her
lips against his neck, the way she had felt in his arms. She
had yielded to him so easily, and the taste of her mouth...

Dear God, this was worse than ever. The primitive,
purely masculine urge to slam on the brakes, gather her up
in his arms and kiss her senseless was one he could subdue
only with the utmost determination. Concentrate on what
you're doing, you fool!

'Are you all right?'

Hell, had something of his thoughts shown in his face?

Or, worse, in his breathing or other, more obvious parts of his body?

'I mean, it must be a terrible strain for you having to drive in this after…'

After your accident. She didn't complete the sentence but let it hang in the air with both of them knowing exactly what was in her mind.

'Perhaps I could take over for a while.'

'No way, sunshine!'

Just the thought was enough to drive everything else from his mind. The heated sensations of a moment earlier subsided so quickly that it was as if he had just opened a window, letting in a blast of the arctic air outside.

'I spent a lot of money on this car. I have no desire to see it nose-down in a ditch!'

'Under normal conditions I am a careful and perfectly competent driver.' Her tone was icy enough to lower the temperature in the car by several degrees. 'But this—' one slim hand gestured towards the swirling blanket of snow that surrounded them '—can hardly be described as "normal".'

'And anyone who deserved the accolade of "careful" driver would have thought more than twice about setting out in weather like this in the first place.'

She hadn't liked that. Her breath hissed through her teeth in fury.

'That has to be the most blatant case of a particularly grubby pot calling a kettle black I've heard in a long time! Might I point out to you that *you* were on the road too? And, as you were clearly nowhere near as far away from home as I was, you would have had the advantage of being able to judge the weather more accurately before you left. It wasn't even snowing when I set out!'

'Nor was it when I left the house!' Sean returned sharply. 'Though I have to admit that I wish it had been. That way I would have had the perfect excuse not to venture out.'

And the perfect excuse to refuse Pete's request. The perfect reason not to go out on what he firmly believed was a

wild-goose chase. He had never held out any real hope that
his brother's ex-fiancée would put in an appearance at the
Night Owl, let alone that he would recognise her, be able
to strike up a conversation and persuade her to come back
home with him.

In fact he had been so convinced of the impossibility of
the task that he hadn't even bothered to order a meal, opting
instead for just a pot of delicious coffee. It had barely been
delivered to his table when the gathering darkness outside,
the grey, lowering skies, had alerted him to the advent of
the wild winter storm that had persisted ever since.

If Annie Elliot had any sense she would never try to
travel in this, he had decided, paying his bill hastily and
setting out for home while it was safe to drive. He had still
not worked out whether it had been good luck or bad that
had resulted in his coming on the silver Renault as he had.

But fate had decided that he would, and that there at the
wheel, tall, dark and every bit as beautiful as his lovelorn
brother had described her, was Miss Heartbreaker Elliot
herself, dazed and off balance and only too willing to be
befriended and taken to his home.

'And of course then you wouldn't have had to lumber
yourself with me!' The girl's indignant voice dragged his
thoughts back to the present.

'I never said—'

'You didn't have to *say* anything! But you've made it
blatantly obvious that you would have been a lot happier
if someone else had come along and rescued me so that
you wouldn't have been obliged to do it. Well, you needn't
worry! I don't want to be stuck with you any more than
you do with me.'

'I couldn't agree more.'

It was expelled on a sigh of exasperation. Damn Pete for
getting him involved in all this, and damn her too...

For what? For being so beautiful that any man would
want her? So lovely that he only had to look at her to burn
with desire?

And she knew it, damn her! She had only just left his

brother, having tossed his ring back in his face, and she already had a new man lined up. And yet she hadn't been able to resist trying it on with *him* in the first five minutes.

She had set out to entice him like some little alley cat, displaying her body in the clinging dress, writhing so seductively against him. And he knew why.

She'd recognised him, hadn't she? Even used his name as familiarly as if they were old friends. It happened so often now that he'd become inured to it. People saw not the real man but a myth created by the medium in which he worked. To the public at large he was simply a face on a TV screen, a glossy photograph in a magazine—that hated thing, a 'pin-up'.

'Well, the best thing is for you to let me use your phone as soon as we get inside. I'll call the garage and—'

'I think not.' Cold, controlled rage turned his voice into a blade of ice slashing through her words.

Forget Pete, and keeping her here until his brother could come and plead with her to take him back! She wasn't worth it. She'd take the poor kid's heart and use it as a toy until she was tired of it, and then she'd snap it in two and toss it aside without even bothering to look where it landed.

Women like this one were just predatory spiders, waiting for the next poor sucker of a fly who foolishly wandered into their carefully spun webs. Marnie had been a mistress of the art as well. But Marnie was out of his life now, thank God. Out of his life and flaunting her brand-new wedding ring and the rich husband to go with it.

But he could use his own experience to teach this lady a much needed lesson. He'd play along with her for now, let her think she had him hooked, and then, just as she enjoyed her triumph, he'd show her that she couldn't play fast and loose with people's feelings.

'You're not going to get away that easily.'

'"Get away"?' For the first time it seemed that her confidence had slipped. A seam of anxiety ran through her repetition of his words.

He'd better take things more carefully. It would do no

good at all to frighten her off right at the start. Far better to lull her into a false sense of security at first, and only reveal his hand when she had no hope of escape.

So he turned a wide smile in her direction and concentrated on making his tone light and friendly.

'See sense, sweetheart! If the garage tow-truck would have found it difficult to reach you earlier, it will be damn near impossible now. They'd need a snow-plough to get through this. We're grounded—stuck together for the duration—so we'll have to make the best of it.'

CHAPTER THREE

'WE'RE here.'

Leah registered Sean's comment, and the fact that the car had slowed, only vaguely. She was grateful for the fact that the nightmare of a journey was over, but only now was it beginning to dawn on her that the tension that had gripped her had more to do with the man beside her than the more obvious danger of the blizzard raging outside.

Her nerves felt stretched tight, as if some cruel hand had gripped them and twisted them hard. Was she imagining things, or had Sean's words been laced with a dark element of threat?

Certainly his declaration that 'You're not going to get away that easily' had sounded ominous. But when she'd queried it he had dismissed her concern with an easy answer and an even easier smile. Though that smile had failed to convince, she admitted, drawing in a sharp, uncomfortable breath.

'You don't look very impressed.'

The lightness of his tone made a nonsense of her feelings.

'Oh, I'm sorry.' With an effort she forced herself to focus on the house before her, or at least on the little she could see through the thickly whirling snow. 'It's just it's not exactly what I was expecting.'

That much was true at least. Small and square, with its grey stone blending in with the wintry surroundings to give it an almost ethereal quality, the cottage was far more basic, more workmanlike than she had anticipated.

'It's not very Sean Gallagher, is it?' her nervousness pushed her to ask.

Immediately all the light vanished from his face, his

34

smile fading and his lips compressing to a cold, thin slash in his face.

'You shouldn't equate the publicity I get with the reality,' he declared, each word cold and clipped, and in a sudden rush of inspiration she suddenly realised just what was wrong.

'I'm sorry, I didn't mean to imply that you were like the part you play.'

A dismissive shrug lifted the powerful shoulders under the fine wool of his jacket.

'It's a common mistake. People see me in a role every week and they tend to assume that role is me.'

And he didn't like that assumption one little bit. It was stamped into every line on his face. Which was why he had seemed so prickly, so downright hostile at moments during their journey.

She had made it plain that she had recognised him from the first; she had been in no state to hide anything from him. And, being used to people reacting to his screen persona rather than the real one, he had written her off as one of his lovesick fans who would do anything for a single glance from their idol's brilliant blue eyes.

But while her blood seemed to curdle in her veins at the thought of being so carelessly pigeonholed, a part of Leah's mind recognised that this fact could actually be her salvation. If Sean saw her simply as an empty-headed worshipper, he would assume that her actions earlier had been the result of excitement at coming face to face with him so unexpectedly.

So, while she couldn't explain, even to herself, just what had possessed her to kiss him, perhaps it was better that way. She couldn't face the prospect of him probing deeper into matters that had already severely rocked her sense of mental balance.

'Well, are we going to make a move, or do you intend to sit here all night until we end up deep-frozen? Here's the key...'

He tossed it at her as she gathered up her handbag, already pushing his own door open.

'Leave the door open. I'll be right behind you when I've got your case.'

The freezing blast of icy air in her face was enough to put wings on Leah's feet. Slipping and sliding, she dashed for the cottage porch, grateful for even the minimal shelter it provided.

Ramming the key into the lock, she turned it with frantic haste, pushing open the door and stumbling into the stone-flagged hallway with a sigh of relief.

True to his word, Sean was close behind her. Dumping her case on the floor, he slammed the door shut behind him as soon as he was over the threshold.

Like Leah, he had already acquired a fine coating of snow on his head and shoulders, the white flakes brilliant and delicate against the darkness. They even, with hearts-stopping effect, clung to the thick black lashes that framed his stunning sapphire eyes.

'The kitchen's through there…'

He waved a hand towards the end of the hall as he stamped his feet to clear the snow from his shoes, shaking himself like some large, powerful animal, spattering her with the cold drops of moisture that spun from his hair.

'The stove will still be banked down, so it should be warm, and you'll need…'

The words trailed off into silence as his eyes met her widened gaze, caught and held.

Why couldn't she move? Leah berated herself. She must look so foolish—and so disgustingly vulnerable—staring at him like this. Why couldn't she just pull off her coat and head in the direction he had indicated?

But it seemed as if her feet were rooted to the spot. She felt as if every cell in her body, every nerve-ending, was sharply attuned to some elemental magnetism that emanated from the man at her side. Any awareness of the rest of her surroundings seemed to have blurred and faded from her sight, so that there was only him and that potent tug of need which had formed in the deepest, most primitive part of her being.

If he had looked big and strong outside, in the space of the countryside, then now he appeared impossibly so—dark and powerful, the confines of the small hallway dominated by the height and breadth of him. His lean, strong body seemed too vital, too forceful to be restricted by its narrow space, its cosy domesticity.

He was more at one with the wild elements outside, as untamed as the wind that buffeted the stone walls of the cottage and came howling down the chimneys.

Because her attention was so firmly fixed on him, she knew the exact moment that the change began. She saw how his long body stiffened, freezing in the act of shrugging out of his coat. She saw the sudden darkening of his eyes, the burning black obliterating the rich blue. With her hearing made acute by heightened sensitivity, she caught the change in his breathing, the faint sound as he swallowed deeply.

'This is the first time I've seen you in the light,' he said, and his voice was strangely husky, raw-edged, as if it had not been used for some time. 'Your eyes—they're almost purple, the colour of pansies.'

'They're like Elizabeth Taylor's, everyone always says,' Leah responded, hearing the words and yet feeling unaware of having actually produced them. 'But of course I don't really look like her. My hair isn't black, for one thing.'

Her lips felt disturbingly dry, and she wet them nervously with the tip of her tongue, then froze as she saw his dark gaze drop to follow the tiny, betraying movement. The intensity of his stare made her heart kick in her chest. Suddenly she saw the gesture from his point of view, realising the unconscious provocation it had offered.

'I prefer your hair colour,' he murmured. 'That sort of sable-brown is much softer. Though right now it's dark enough to pass for black.'

His hand came out to stroke one of the sodden strands that lay over her shoulder. His touch was very gentle, but with every cell in her body hypersensitive to the pull of his physical appeal Leah had to fight the instinctive reaction that almost had her jumping away like a nervous cat.

'Liz Taylor is regarded as one of the world's greatest beauties.'

'Fishing for compliments?'

A slow smile, its sensual appeal lethal to her composure, curled the corners of that beautiful mouth.

'Believe me, you don't need to. You must know that you are an exceptionally lovely woman, the sort any man would be proud to have on his arm. Or...' the smooth voice deepened deliberately '...in his bed.'

Those vivid eyes held Leah's hypnotically, sapphire locked with violet in spellbound isolation from which she was totally unable to break free. She no longer saw the flawed beauty of the damaged side of his face, the raw, red marks that marred the sculpted line of his bones, the plane of his cheek. She was aware only of the glossy darkness of his hair, the unexpected softness of his mouth—and, above and beyond anything else, the burning, mesmeric force of his gaze.

'I...'

It was all she could manage before her voice failed her completely. Twice she swallowed deeply, opened her mouth, but each time no sound came out, her ability to speak having deserted her.

The silence in the small house was so profound that his breathing seemed unnaturally loud. She could almost sense each exhalation as a warm caress across her skin, raising goosebumps of reaction all over her body.

'I...?' said Sean softly, lifting the single syllable on a questioning note.

His smile, the light in his eyes, seemed to say that he knew exactly what she was thinking and that he shared those thoughts. Shared the shivering sense of awareness, the heightened sensitivity to everything around them. With infinite slowness his head tilted, came nearer.

The tiny movement was enough to have Leah closing

her eyes in panic, but only for a second. Suddenly fearful that he might interpret her reaction as an invitation to kiss her, she forced them open again, focusing determinedly on a single dark lock that had broken free from the sleeked back smoothness of his snow-soaked hair so that it fell forward over one straight black eyebrow.

'Sean...'

As she spoke a single drop of molten snow slid, hung, and finally fell from his hair onto his skin, trailing slowly down towards the corner of his eye. Acting purely instinctively, Leah reached out and stopped it with a gentle fingertip, slowly retracing its path to wipe the cold dampness from his skin.

'Don't!'

Sharp and hard, it was a rough command that stilled the movement at once. Her eyes flew to his in a look of stunned confusion.

'But it would have gone into your eye!'

Almost all the blue had disappeared from his iris, she realised. In its place was just a pool of black, with the tiniest rim of colour at its outer edge.

'It might have stung.'

'And you would hate to see me suffer even the slightest distress?'

The mockery in his voice was at odds with the heavy-lidded sensuality of his gaze, the warmth that softened his mouth.

As Leah watched with disbelieving fascination that smile grew, and with a slow, indolent movement he turned his head slightly into the hand that still rested against his face. She felt the heat of his skin, warm satin underneath her fingertips, but rougher lower down, where the day's growth of beard abraded her palm.

She couldn't hold back a soft murmur of response, a murmur that turned into a choking cry as she felt the new warmth of his lips against her palm. His soft kiss sent a burning reaction like a wild electric shock crackling through every nerve in her arm.

Drawing in a sharp breath, she snatched her hand away, cradling it against her breasts as if it had actually been scorched. Above it, her eyes were wide and dark as pansies in shocked reaction.

'Why did you do that?'

'Why?' he echoed thickly. 'Because I wanted to. Because it felt right, and I enjoyed it. And because...'

Blue eyes smoky with unconcealed desire, he took a step closer, then another. He reached out for her hand, lifting it once more to his lips.

'Because...'

With his dark eyes still on her face, he traced the shape of her palm in soft, brief kisses, adding the touch of his tongue as he moved up her index finger. He planted a final kiss right on its tip before turning it towards her, letting it rest on her parted mouth as if to deliver the caress back to her. Leah shuddered faintly as she tasted the mixture of herself and Sean on her own skin.

'Because you wanted it too, didn't you?'

'Oh, God!' She choked the words out, unable to respond to his soft-voiced question.

'Didn't you?'

She could deny it, but what would be the point? She knew he was right, and he knew it too. He could read it in her eyes, in their darkness that matched the intensity of his own, in the heightened breathing that brought hot colour to her cheeks and to the creamy breasts that rose and fell rapidly under the tight-fitting bodice of her dress.

'Yes...'

It was a sigh of resignation, of defeat, but as soon as she had spoken she felt strangely liberated, as if some great weight had dropped from her shoulders.

'Yes,' she repeated more firmly, conviction lifting her voice. 'Yes! Oh, yes!'

'I knew it.'

A soft thud as the coat he had been in the process of removing finally hit the floor was the last thing Leah was aware of as Sean reached for her, his arms closing round her and hauling her hard up against the lean length of his body. Rough hands in her hair pulled her head back, lifting her face to his, and her mouth was captured in a wild, bruising kiss. With a tiny moan she opened her lips to him, her tongue tangling with his in instant response.

Her groan was matched by an identical one from Sean himself, and then he was kissing her again, but very differently this time. He took her lips hotly, greedily, snatching at her mouth, her face, her neck, like a man who had been starved for a long, long time and was now presented with such an array of dishes that he didn't know which one to taste first.

One strong hand held the back of her head, keeping her face imprisoned against his, while the other tugged at her already loosened coat, wrenching it from her body and discarding it carelessly beside his own. Inserting one powerful thigh between both of hers, he pushed her backwards until she came hard up against the wall, trapped by the strength of his body.

The heat of his skin reached her through the fine velvet of her dress, and even the heavy denim of his jeans could not conceal the burning evidence of his desire for her as he crushed it against the cradle of her hips. He inched her legs further apart and she yielded willingly, sighing aloud once more as the pressure at the juncture of her legs inflamed the heated need his caresses had created there.

'Sean...'

His name was a moan of yearning, of hunger, and his raw-edged, shaky laughter in response told her that he recognised the craving that had her in its grip. Recognised it and shared it in every way.

'I don't know how this happened.' It was a rough mutter, thick and raw against her skin. 'I only know there was no way of avoiding it. That it was inevitable from the moment I first set eyes on you. When— Dear God!'

A shudder ran through his long body.

'I thought you were dead, or badly hurt! I thought—'

'Sean!' Hungry impatience made her break into his words. 'Will you shut up and kiss me?'

'With the greatest pleasure!'

He did more than kiss her. His mouth seemed to have turned into a finely tuned instrument of pleasure, touching, caressing, nibbling, occasionally administering tiny, sharp, demanding bites down her throat and on to the creamy skin exposed by the neckline of her dress.

And all the time his hands were busy too, moving over her body, cupping and holding her breasts. His thumbs circled the shape of her nipples, rubbing softly, bringing them into tight, excited life beneath the clinging fabric.

Leah's head was thrown back, her eyes closed. She was on fire, every inch of her body burning up, every cell ablaze with need. Her urgent fingers pushed aside the navy sweater, sliding over the broad leather belt at his waist, a choking cry of delight escaping her as her fingertips encountered the heated softness of his skin.

Fingers spread wide, she smoothed her hands outwards and upwards over the strong lines of his chest, feeling the powerful muscles bunch and jerk under her caress. Her sensuous exploration found the rasp of body hair, the tiny, hard buds of his male nipples, and delighted in all the differences between his physique and her own.

Beneath her touch she sensed the heavy pounding of his heart, and with a deliberately sinuous, almost feline movement she slid her hips against the hardness of his arousal. Her smile was one of triumph as she sensed his heartbeat accelerate dramatically.

'I think we'd be more comfortable in another room,' Sean muttered against her cheek, having dragged his mouth from hers with obvious reluctance.

'You have a point.'

Her words were almost unintelligible, but the undercurrent of shaken laughter told its own story.

With her arms linked around his neck, he half carried, half walked her towards the nearest room, kicking open the door before manoeuvring her inside. Leah had a brief glimpse of a Victorian-style tiled fireplace and large, squashy chairs covered in a rich bronze velvet before she was swung off her feet and deposited on the softness of the settee, Sean coming down on top of her.

'Better?' he enquired unevenly, his breathing as ragged as if he had just completed a marathon.

'*Much* better,' Leah assured him with a lazy smile, writhing languorously beneath his imprisoning weight.

'Now perhaps I can kiss you properly.'

When Leah opened her mouth to demand to know precisely what he had been doing before, if not kissing her 'properly', he promptly took the opportunity to prove exactly what he meant. The thrust and movement of his tongue was a deliberate attempt to tease and tantalise her with the promise of how a more intimate invasion of her body would feel.

The hunger that had built with each touch, each caress, was now raging out of control. It pulsed through every nerve-end, making her twist violently beneath him. She needed to touch him more intimately, wanted to feel his hot skin against hers, wanted his hands on her own body.

'You're wearing too many clothes,' she muttered in mock petulance, tugging at the navy sweater with impatient fingers.

'I could say the same about you.'

'Mmm, so you could.' Leah moved her hips provocatively. 'And this dress is far too tight.'

'Is that a fact? Well, I think I could help you there.'

The Lycra that made her dress cling so closely also made it easy for him to ease the top down from her shoulders, the bra beneath as swiftly discarded. Pausing only to peel off his jumper and toss it aside, Sean came back to her again, dragging her up against him and deliberately moving his chest against the peaking tips of her nipples. His smile grew into a wide grin of triumph as he heard her sigh of uninhibited pleasure at the sensation of the roughness of his body hair against their tight sensitivity.

'You are one sexy lady,' he murmured against her skin,

trailing hot kisses down from the smooth roundness of one shoulder to the pink-flushed curves of her breasts. Slowly, tormentingly, his mouth moved lower, so that she was whimpering with need before it finally closed over one throbbing peak, drawing it into its moist heat.

'Oh, God!'

Leah's body arched upwards convulsively, her head flung back in total abandon as she offered herself to the delicious sensation. Sean's gentle tugging at her breast sent a pulse of white-hot excitement straight from its tip down to the very centre of her femininity.

'Don't stop!' she begged, and felt his laughter feather warmly across her flesh.

'I don't intend to.'

His hands were tugging her skirt upwards, exposing the lacy tops of her stockings, the frivolous fastenings of her suspender belt. Automatically Leah raised herself to help him.

When his questing fingers slid over her hip-bones and under the wisp of silk that was the only flimsy barrier left between him and her most intimate core, she cried out sharply, the sound of her voice clashing with the soft chiming of a clock somewhere in the room.

'God, but you're ready for me,' he breathed. 'So ready. I can see that making love to you just once is never going to be enough for me. I'd want to do it again…'

His fingers tangled in the damp curls, probed gently for a second, making her move uncontrollably.

'And again…'

Each word coincided with the stroke of the clock in the corner, creating a rhythm that forced itself through the fevered haze inside Leah's head. It pounded against her brain, refusing to be pushed away until, in spite of herself, she found she was counting along with them.

Six… Seven

'And *again!*'

Eight… Nine…

Nine! The final stroke slashed into her consciousness like a blade of ice, incising the passion from her thoughts with a single blow.

Nine o'clock! There was something— She had promised— Oh, God, what was happening to her?

'No!'

It was a cry of shocked distress, so sharp, so shaken that even in his state of fevered desire Sean heard it and paused in confusion. Blue eyes dark and glazed with passion went to her face.

'Sweetheart...'

'I said no!'

She wrenched herself up into a half-sitting position, shaking fingers going to her exposed breasts, then down to her skirt in an ineffectual attempt to cover herself. But when she realised that Sean's hands still lingered intimately at the top of her thighs she pushed them away with a violence that clearly surprised him.

What had she done? How could she have let this happen? How could she have been so foolish as to let things go this far?

Nine o'clock! She had promised Andy she would phone him at nine to let him know she had arrived safely at her mother's house.

But she wasn't at her mother's, or anywhere near it. And she certainly wasn't *safe*! She was here, with a man she had met only a couple of hours before—a man she knew nothing about except for his appearances on her television set, a man she had let...

'No!'

This time it was a wail of distress and shame. How *could* she have forgotten? How could she have let him drive it from her mind?

'This mustn't happen! It's wrong! So very wrong! I'm— I'm engaged to someone else!'

She didn't know what she had expected his response to be. A protest, at least. Or perhaps some attempt at seductive persuasion—a few sultry kisses, a murmured, Forget him, darling, he's history. You and I are meant to be together.

Instead, the man above her turned white with shock. The words were barely out of her mouth before he had snatched his hands away from her so swiftly that she might just have told him she was infected with some appalling disease.

With a violent imprecation he levered himself up and away from her, his long body jack-knifing off the settee before he swung violently away towards the window.

'Engaged!' she heard him fling at her with savage fury. 'Of course you're bloody engaged! You're not free, you deceitful little bitch!'

'Sean…I'm sorry.'

It was all she could manage. A devastating ache had taken possession of her body so that she felt as if she was bruised all over. Her exposed breasts, their nipples still swollen from his attentions, were agonisingly sensitive to the cold air that had taken the place of his warm, caressing mouth. But there was a deeper, racking sense of loss that twisted her insides into bitter knots of despair.

'I'm really sorry.'

'*You're* sorry!' He whirled round, blue eyes blazing in the white mask that was his face, livid marks of rage etched around his nose and mouth. 'You're *sorry*! How the hell do you think I feel? I knew—'

Once more he swore, viciously and fluently, a clenched fist slamming against his forehead as he shook his dark head in furious disbelief.

'Of course you're bloody well engaged! But that didn't stop you, did it? *Did it?* So tell me…'

Abruptly his voice had changed, but Leah found the deadly softness of the question even more unnerving than the violence of the fury that had gone before. The febrile glitter in his eyes terrified her, so that she shrank back against the cushions, recoiling as if his words had been actual blows.

'Tell me, you greedy little two-timing bitch, just how many do you want?'

As Leah frowned her incomprehension, unable to collect her shattered thoughts enough to even see what he was driving at, let alone answer him, he repeated the question. But this time he expanded it so that there could be no doubt as to exactly what insult he had meant to imply by it.

'How many, my darling? Are you so insatiable that even *two* men are not enough for you?'

moving in, had almost answered him. He had raised his questing hand tantalisingly to caress the warm curve of her breast as he, 'exactly what he'd been talking about in his sleep, 'Do you want any tea sir? Are you going to be in that even, you got sick?'

CHAPTER FOUR

'I'M ENGAGED to someone else!'

The words pounded against Sean's skull, making him want to shake his head violently to drive away their ominous sound. Each repetition seemed to twist his conscience even more painfully than before.

'I'm engaged.'

Of course she was bloody well engaged! And he knew only too well just who her fiancé was—or rather had been, until a few short hours before.

But, engaged or not, she was still off-limits. More than anyone, he knew how much this woman meant *to his brother*.

'Sean...'

With a violent movement he averted his eyes from where she lay on the settee, her long legs pale against the bronze cushions. Her breasts...

'Cover yourself up!'

His voice was harsh, thickened with the disgust he felt. He couldn't believe that he had ever found her beautiful, that she still seemed that way to him. Instead, he felt that, in some twisted reversal of the old fairy story, she should have become foul and disgusting in his eyes, as if he had kissed a princess and seen her turn into a grossly repellent, poisonous toad.

But even worse than that was the guilt that assailed him. The knowledge that he had let himself be enticed into her carefully baited feminine trap. He had been so base, so foolish. Even now his body still throbbed with unappeased desire, making him ache right to his very soul.

God, he'd thought he was a rational, reasonable sort of

man, but it seemed that he was just as easily led by his
most primitive instincts as anyone else.

'I said, cover yourself up!' he flung at her when she
didn't move. 'Do you think I want to see you lying there,
flaunting yourself?'

That got through to her. Those amazing eyes flashed furiously as she swung her legs to the floor, adjusting her
dress as she did so.

'I was *not* flaunting myself! What is this, Sean? Are you
trying to claim that you had no part in what just happened?
That I just led you on, and you were the poor, innocent
party in my—'

'Not innocent, no!' Sean flashed, swinging round to face
her again, and then immediately wishing he hadn't.

With her brown hair tumbled around her shoulders, her
eyes wide and dark, she looked like some innocent schoolgirl. That effect was heightened by the fact that her make-
up had all but vanished, her lipstick wiped off.

Kissed off, his conscience reminded him, making him
want to groan aloud at the memory of how that soft mouth
had felt underneath his own, how willingly it had opened
to the pressure of his lips, the taste of it still lingering on
his tongue.

'We were equals in desire, yes. But you were the one
who didn't tell the truth. You lied...'

'No! I never said anything that wasn't true!'

'By omission, then!' Sean snapped. 'It amounts to the
same thing. You were the one who neglected to inform me
of the existence of your fiancé until it was almost too late!'

'I know.'

To his consternation, Sean came close to regretting the
harshness of his tirade when he saw her reaction. Saw the
betraying shimmer in her eyes, the way her small white
teeth dug into the softness of her lower lip. Close, but not
close enough. Because as his words died away he came
hard up against the other unsavoury fact that his anger had
pushed to the back of his mind.

It wasn't just Pete that she had been prepared to betray.

Not only had she walked out on his brother, leaving him emotionally shattered, but she had already transferred her affections, such as they were, to another man entirely.

'But it isn't exactly a firm engagement. I mean—'

'I don't want to know what you mean!' Sean roared furiously, clenching his hands tightly and shoving them into the pockets of his jeans, not trusting himself to resist the temptation to use them.

Deep inside, he was prey to a darkly primitive urge to grab her and shake her to within an inch of her life, and the realisation that he could be so totally uncivilised, in thought at least, shocked him to the core of his being.

He knew only too well just how far from 'firm' her engagement was. Hadn't he had to pick up the pieces of his brother, metaphorically at least, that she had left behind? Pete had been shattered, close to breaking point if the rawness of his voice had been anything to go by. But this little madam had flounced off to her new lover without even a backward glance.

'To my mind any engagement is as binding as it comes, second only to actual marriage vows. So what was I to you? A little diversion while *en route* to something more interesting?'

'No! Never that. I—I just don't know what came over me.'

'Oh, I do, darling.'

He laced the endearment with an acid that turned it into the worst form of insult, and knew that it had hit home as he saw her wince unhappily. The surprisingly vulnerable reaction did uncomfortable things to his guts, and he had to clamp down hard on the weak response in order to be able to glare into those wide violet eyes.

'I know exactly what got into you. It's a very simple, straightforward word. A four-letter word, in fact—in both senses of the term. A basic word for a very basic feeling. I'll spell it out for you, shall I, sweetheart? It's called lust, pure and simple—though there was nothing in the remotest bit *pure* about your behaviour just now.'

'And you, I suppose, were inspired by the purest love?' Leah flashed up at him. That dark, proud head had gone back, her chin coming up defiantly. Even the pansy eyes burned with molten-gold flares of anger.

'Never that!'

'Never that!' she echoed, a new contempt shading her retort.

That earlier disconcerting vulnerability had been stripped away, and in its place was a very different persona. Sean strongly suspected that at last he was seeing the real woman, the one who had been hidden under the carefully cultivated veneer of defencelessness.

He was forced to wonder whether she had ever shown this other, harder side of herself to Pete. Privately he doubted it. His brother had always described his fiancée in terms of sweetness and light. But then Pete had always been a sucker for a beautiful face and a soft voice.

As he had himself, a brutally realistic voice at the back of his thoughts reminded him sharply.

'No, never that!' she repeated. 'Your motivation was every bit as *base* as you accuse me of being.'

The acid in her attack matched his own in bitterness.

'But I suppose it's fine for a *man* to feel such things! A woman who feels physical desire—sexual passion—isn't quite nice, quite feminine, is she? And if she dares to show the way that she feels, then she's what—an insatiable tart?'

So she hadn't liked his own outspoken accusation, Sean registered with grim satisfaction.

'You're the one who's engaged to someone else. And in my book, anyone—man or woman—who indulges in "sexual passion"..' Deliberately he quoted her own words back at her, each word seeming to be formed in ice.

As he spoke, Marnie's face floated before his mind's eye and wouldn't be pushed away, no matter how hard he tried. His efforts to drive the unwanted image from his thoughts made his tone even harsher as he went on.

'While committed to someone else, whether firmly or otherwise, is—yes—guilty of behaviour of the lowest kind.'

That had caught her on the raw, he noted with some satisfaction, seeing the yellow flames burning in those amazing eyes.

'And what gives you the right to be so bloody sanctimonious about everything?'

She was ramming on the battered shoes as she spoke, not even looking at her feet, her attention fixed firmly on his face.

'You were no damn— Oh!'

It was a cry of shock. Finding the rough treatment positively the last straw, the elderly leather of her shoes had finally given way, splitting all along the side of the right foot.

'Here!'

Sean's response was instinctive, automatic, as was the way he moved forward. Firm fingers closed over hers, his other hand going to support her elbow as he pulled her upright.

Expecting resistance, he pulled harder than she had obviously anticipated, making her sway against his chest, one of her hands coming up to steady herself on his shoulder.

The sensual mixture of flowers and spice that was her perfume assailed his senses, the air it floated on seeming to be still warm from the heat of her flushed skin. The soft brush of her velvet-covered breasts against the wall of his chest was almost more than he could bear.

'Oh, God!'

He didn't know if he had actually said the words out loud or simply let the exclamation escape inside his thoughts. But, a second later, looking into the pansy-dark pools of her eyes told him that no words needed to have been spoken.

She knew anyway. Knew that he had only to touch her and his body reacted, tightening, swelling in a need he could not disguise. But this time there was no matching response in her own face, no softening in her body, only a freezing into stiff coldness that had more of a sobering effect than the coldest of showers had ever done in the past.

'I'm fine now, thank you,' she said, and the clipped, curt delivery made a nonsense of the last two polite words. 'So if you'll just…'

Deliberately she let the purple gaze drop to where his hand still held hers. It was as if the ice in her tone had been injected into his bloodstream so that he couldn't release her quickly enough, unable to bear the burning pain of being so completely frozen out.

'And now, seeing as it's only too plain that you don't want me here any more than I want to stay, perhaps you'll let me phone a garage.'

For a split second or two Sean was actually tempted. If she could get her car back on the road then she would go, and leave him in peace. He could get himself back under control and rid his mind of the hateful mixture of hunger and guilt that had preyed on him ever since he had first seen her.

But almost immediately he rejected the thought. That wasn't how things were meant to go.

He had promised Pete that he would hold onto this woman until his brother could get here to talk to her, and he planned on keeping that promise. Though when the young fool finally arrived he was fully determined to take him to one side and hand out a few home truths about his so-called fiancée. Pete would hate him for it, but he knew he couldn't live with himself if he let his brother persist in his blind self-delusion.

But until he could do that he had to make sure that she stayed in the cottage. And so…

'Sorry,' he drawled, making it plain he felt no such thing. 'No can do. There's no phone.'

'No phone!' Her consternation was obvious, her eyes wide as she stared round the room, testing the truth of his declaration. 'But there has to be!'

Sean shook his head, privately thanking his lucky stars that the telephone was hidden away in the tiny room the estate agent had described laughably as 'the study', with the door firmly shut.

'But I have to ring—'

'Your fiancé? Or perhaps you have some other poor sucker lined up waiting for a call? Either way, I'm sure they'd be only too pleased to know that you're stranded in some remote cottage with—what was it? God's gift to women?—and no hope of getting out for at least twenty-four hours, if not more.'

'If you must know, I wanted to phone my family. I—'

She broke off, all colour leaching from her cheeks as she registered what he'd said.

'Twenty-four hours! You can't be serious!'

'Never more so, sweetheart. Did you notice anything about the weather on the way here? You couldn't have been totally unaware of the fact that snowfall like that will block the roads in minutes, let alone the hour or so we've been inside. But, no—I suppose you had too much on your mind to register that.'

Deliberately he let his eyes slide to the settee, lingering on the crushed and disordered cushions where only minutes before they had lain together, limbs intimately entwined. Once more he felt a twist of reaction torment his nerves at the recollection of her unrestrained response.

'But if you doubt my word you only have to look out of the window to see the truth of the situation.'

'We can't be trapped!'

She went to the window, staring out at the white drifts piling up against the walls, the skeletal outlines of the trees, branches weighted down close to breaking point. Her expression was almost as bleak as the landscape outside.

'We can.'

Abruptly he lost interest in the dark teasing, turning away from her and reaching for his discarded sweater, pulling it on with a rough, jerky movement.

'Face it, lady, we're stuck here together for as long as this snow takes to clear. And, while I'm no more pleased about the situation than you are, I'm forced to accept the fact that I can see no possible alternative. If you're wise you'll do the same.'

'I don't seem to have any choice.'

Her voice was unexpectedly subdued, and as she spoke he caught the faint shiver that shook her feminine frame. Immediately his conscience pricked him uncomfortably.

'You're cold. Look, why don't I show you to your room and you can change into something warmer and more comfortable?'

'Something less tarty, don't you mean?' she flashed back. 'Something less characteristic of the woman you think I am.'

'If the dress fits,' he murmured sardonically, smiling straight into her indignant face. 'Look, lady, all I mean is that we're stuck here, whether we like it or not, so we might as well make the best of things. I think we could communicate more—rationally—if you wore something a little less provocative.'

Certainly he would feel more in control if he wasn't confronted at every turn by the soft smoothness of her flesh, the peachy bloom of those rounded shoulders, the cleavage beneath. If he didn't have to see the way the velvet dress clung lovingly to every curve, see the hellishly short skirt that exposed those long, long legs...

'And you'll be able to stop drooling!'

'You'd also feel better if you were warmer,' Sean persisted, refusing to rise to her bait.

Was he really so obvious? Did what he thought show in his eyes every time he looked at her? Or was it just that she recognised the hunger he felt because she had been in its grip too, and possibly still felt its power?

'This cottage isn't centrally heated, and you got soaked while you were outside. You'd be much more comfortable in something dry and clean.'

'We both would,' she put in unexpectedly.

When he frowned his surprise at her interjection she gestured silently with one hand, drawing his attention to the way that his jeans were still darkened from his knees to his ankles where the snow had melted. In the heat of events since their arrival at the cottage he hadn't even registered the fact that his clothes were as wet as her own.

'We both would,' he agreed soberly. 'You must be chilled to the bone. So why don't you have a shower to warm yourself through and then get changed? There's plenty of hot water. I left the immersion heater on while I was out.'

Practicality helped. It distracted him from the blatant carnality of his thoughts, imposed control on a situation he had feared was rapidly running away from him.

'And while you do that I'll get the fire going again and sort out something to eat. How does that sound?'

'Wonderful!' It came out on a sigh, her voice surprisingly weak, and she passed a hand briefly across her eyes as if suddenly very tired.

'Are you OK?'

For a moment genuine concern sharpened his voice, only to fade again as swiftly as it had come when he saw her suddenly snap to attention again, clearly ready to repulse any move he made to help her.

'I'm fine.'

'Are you sure?' If he was honest, she didn't look it. Her face was colourless, her eyes seeming too big above her pallid cheeks. 'You could still be in shock—the after-effects of the accident.'

'I'm *fine*. And if I am in shock it's not the accident that caused it. So if you'll just tell me which room I can have...'

Sean didn't care for her coolly dismissive tone, and he liked even less the way she looked down her nose at him, as if he was something particularly nasty and foul-smelling that had just crawled out from under a stone. But he clamped his jaw tight shut on an angry response.

'This way.'

In the hall he picked up her bag and led the way up the steep, creaking staircase to the narrow landing at the top.

'Bathroom,' he announced, flinging open the nearest of the three doors. 'My bedroom—and yours—'

Then he caught the way she was looking at him.

'What the hell is it now? Oh, I see!'

It was almost as if he could read her mind, so clearly were her thoughts stamped on that fine-boned face.

'You didn't really believe that I would provide separate bedrooms, is that it? Well, you don't have to worry about that, sweetheart. Believe me, you're perfectly safe. I have no designs on your virtue at all.'

'My virtue?' Her tone was taut, but she seemed to be having to make an effort to inject it with the sort of bite that had been there before. 'I didn't think you believed I had any.'

'My opinion of you is irrelevant.'

Unable to trust himself not to respond to her provocation if he stayed any longer, he dropped her case onto the narrow bed in the far corner of the room he had allocated to her, heedless of whether it landed safely or not, and turned for the stairs.

'There are clean towels in the airing cupboard in the bathroom,' he tossed at her. 'Help yourself.'

'Perhaps it's your own virtue that you're afraid might be threatened.'

Her taunt floated down the stairs after him, the malicious mockery in her tone making a nonsense of his earlier worry that she might be feeling unwell.

Downstairs, he was thankful that the physical activity needed to collect coal, lay and light the fire was a welcome distraction from other, less acceptable thoughts. It proved a much needed antidote to the fizzing electrical energy that seemed to be burning in his blood, keeping him permanently on edge.

It was just anger that made him feel this way, he told himself. Anger at the way she had led him on then suddenly applied the brakes so hard that he had practically bruised himself against the force of her rejection.

Anger at the weather that now kept them trapped here together and ensured that Pete, even supposing he'd got himself sobered up fast, would not be able to come and collect her for twenty-four hours or more.

Anger at his brother's fiancée for being the sort of cold, heartless bitch who could leap into one man's bed when she had only just left another victim broken-hearted—and all the time having yet a third lover dangling on a string.

'Damn her!' He slammed coal onto the fire with a violence that expressed the force of his feelings. 'Damn her to hell!'

But the real problem was knowing that the full strength of his fury was actually directed at himself. He had known from the start just who this woman was, and yet that hadn't stopped him at all. No thought of Pete had been in his mind when he had kissed that incredibly full, soft mouth, when he had caressed the smooth warmth of her skin, peeled away the clinging velvet dress...

'Oh, God!'

This time he could not hold back the groan of response. He had accused her of feeling nothing more than lust and she had flung the accusation right back in his face. And she had been right.

That was the real trouble. He couldn't even begin to try to deny it. He had wanted her so badly, desired her with a passion that made his body ache just to recall it. He had lusted after her—and he still did.

It should have been easier with her out of the room. He might have thought that then the fire burning in his blood, the throbbing race of his pulse, would slow, gradually fading away. But in fact he felt far worse.

What he should be doing was contacting Pete. The young fool would be desperate to know if his plan had succeeded and if his erstwhile fiancée was safely secured so that he could come and try to talk some sense into her. After all, seeing as he had told Annie that he had no phone, it wouldn't do to have his brother shatter that illusion with a frantic enquiry later. He'd do it now, while she was in the shower.

But the only response from the other end of the line was the infuriating repetition of the engaged tone. Either Pete was pouring out his tale of woe to someone else or he had left the phone off the hook while he sobered himself up. Either way, he would have to leave it for now.

As he crossed the hall again he could hear the sound of the shower, still running in the bathroom upstairs. It was impossible not to think of that water pounding down onto her naked body, not to imagine that white flesh beginning to glow under the heat of it. Impossible not to picture her hands, rich with creamy lather, gliding over the curves of her breasts, sliding down past her waist, over her hips...

'Hell, no!'

With a brutal effort he dragged his mind away from such tormenting images and forced it onto practical matters, hurrying to the kitchen. Coffee first, to warm them both, and then he would think of food.

His concentration was so fierce that he barely registered that the sound of the shower had ceased, didn't hear the soft pad of bare feet across the landing. He was absorbed in peeling and chopping vegetables when a quiet voice spoke behind him.

'Can I do anything to help?'

Sean's hand closed over his knife in convulsive reaction. But that one second of response was all that he allowed himself. Deliberately keeping his face turned away, he shook his head, turning only when he knew that he had his expression and his breathing well under control.

'It's all in hand. It's just something quick and easy.'

Change into something more comfortable, he had said, and she had done just that. But if she had aimed for something less provocative then she most definitely had not succeeded.

The well-worn denim jeans she had on were skintight, clinging to the rounded hips and long legs almost as lovingly as the velvet dress had done. And the lilac sweater picked up and deepened the colour of those stunning eyes, making them look even more brilliant against the magnolia blossom purity of her skin.

With her face entirely free of the artifice of make-up, she looked, if it were possible, even more beautiful than before.

Her long dark hair, still damp from her shower, fell loose in soft waves around her shoulders, the ends just beginning to curl as they dried. She looked at least ten years younger than when he had first seen her, and infinitely more approachable, almost delicately vulnerable, especially when her nose twitched like that.

'Something smells good anyway. Italian?'

'Mmm.'

Hastily he crushed down his weak thoughts, refusing to allow himself to acknowledge how appealing she looked as she inhaled appreciatively.

'Lasagne.'

'Wonderful!' Her smile lit up her face. 'I'm very impressed.'

'Don't be.' Sean was unable to stop himself from responding to her enthusiasm with a grin of his own. 'I have to admit that I didn't make it from scratch. In this case, "quick and easy" means something cooked and frozen by my mother. All I've done is reheat it according to her instructions.'

'You obviously have a very loving mother.'

'She was concerned that, left to myself, I wouldn't eat properly, and she might just have been right.'

'It's been a bad time for you?'

Catching the surprised glance he slanted in her direction, she made a small, appeasing gesture with her hands.

'It's just that you don't strike me as the sort of man who would normally neglect important things like that. And, as you seem pretty self-reliant, I can't believe that you don't really know how to cook.'

Her perspicacity knocked him off balance for a moment, so that before he quite realised it he had told her the truth.

'At one time I admit I was so low that I took very little interest in anything.'

The look in her eyes, a sudden shadow in their violet depths, alerted him to the fact that he had let slip more than he had intended and needed to act hastily to cover his tracks.

'But that gave my mother the perfect opportunity to play doting parent. Through there—' he indicated a door at the far end of the tiny kitchen '—is a freezer stuffed to the gills with enough goodies to feed an army for a month.'

To his relief, she followed his lead.

'Just what you need in weather like this. It is still snowing, I take it?'

'Worse than ever. When I last looked out, the tracks the car had made were already completely covered. We were lucky to make it here at all.'

'And if you hadn't come along to help me I would have been in real trouble,' she said with a faint shudder. 'I really do appreciate your help.'

'I could hardly have left you there,' Sean growled.

It was damnably difficult maintaining this conversation. The trouble was that it seemed just an ordinary exchange of polite trivia, so that anyone looking in from outside would have believed it to be precisely that. But polite and trivial was not at all the way he felt.

Every inch of his body was stretched taut in awareness of her physical presence. In his ears her voice sounded so soft and musical that he felt he could listen to it all night and never tire of the sound. His fingers itched to smooth over those fine-boned shoulders, slide through the glossy brown hair. He was a burning tangle of unease, had a hunger that no food could satisfy, while she looked so cool and composed, totally in control.

And that was the real problem. This was not at all how he wanted her to be, damn her!

He didn't want her to stand there looking as if butter wouldn't melt in her mouth. Not when he could remember how wild she had been in his arms, how gloriously needy and wanton. He didn't want to believe that she could switch from that passion to this control in the space of a few short moments. He wanted her to be as shaken as he had been— as he still was.

'But, all the same, I do appreciate it.'

'No problem.'

The scar on his face ached abominably, and he rubbed at it abstractedly, freezing when he saw her eyes follow the movement.

'Was it because of the accident that you felt so low? Look, are you sure I can't help?'

'You can pour a drink, if you like. That cupboard over there. Wine for me, and whatever you'd like.'

'I'll have the same.'

Her voice was muffled as she reached into the cupboard he had indicated, pulling out a bottle and a couple of glasses. Sean suddenly had the strangest feeling that she was actually trying to make things easier for him. That she was giving him the chance to answer the question in his own time.

'Yes, it was after the accident. For a while I felt pretty disillusioned and had no interest in anything.'

Until he'd heard the words spoken out loud he hadn't believed he was going to say them. He had hardly spoken to anyone about this, let alone a complete stranger.

Perhaps it was something as simple as the fact that she had kept her back to him, concentrating on pouring the wine, that made it easier to tell her.

'"Disillusioned"? That's a strange word to use.'

She was turning back now, holding out a glass to him.

'I could see why you'd feel depressed or downhearted, but disillusioned...'

'You'd understand if you knew the whole story,' Sean muttered cynically.

Oh, damn his bloody big mouth! He'd given her the perfect opportunity to say, Tell me the whole story. And that was something he hadn't done—even to Pete or his mother.

Surprisingly, she didn't pick him up on it. Instead she frowned delicately, a fine line appearing in the space between her arched brows.

'How long ago was this accident? That scar looks pretty recent.'

'You could say that.' His mouth twisted on the words.

'I got out of hospital just over eight weeks ago. I was actually a patient for a fortnight or so.'

'That would explain it.'

She nodded slowly, the violet eyes resting briefly on the damaged side of his face.

'Do you want this wine or not?'

Belatedly Sean realised that she was still holding the glass out to him. He moved forward to take it from her, frowning darkly when he saw the way she jumped as their fingers brushed for a second, the speed with which she stepped backwards, away from him.

'I suppose in time it will fade—become less dramatic.'

'Less horrific, don't you mean?' Sean snarled, still smarting from her nervous reaction. 'Well, I hate to disillusion you, but I'll never look like Inspector Callender, let alone—what was the phrase you used?—God's gift to women, ever again!'

To his consternation she actually looked hurt.

'That wasn't what I meant at all! But I suppose I should have known that's how you'd interpret what I said. After all, your face is your fortune, isn't it? You must hate the idea that you no longer qualify for a place in the top ten sexiest men alive. It really must have dealt your lady-killer image a terrible blow. Is that why you're hiding away up here in this isolated spot?'

For a mindless second Sean's hand tightened round the stem of his glass so convulsively that he was frankly surprised when it didn't snap under the pressure. In the back of his mind he could hear Marnie's voice, taunting him with almost the very same words, and his eyes closed briefly against the memories it brought with it.

'I told you before not to confuse the character I play with reality,' he tossed at her coolly. 'And for your information, I am not "hiding away" anywhere. I had already decided on a couple of months' holiday before the accident. In the circumstances it seemed even more important to take it, in order to ensure that I was fully fit to return to work when the time came.'

As he spoke he was moving to check the food in the cooker, so he didn't see her reaction to his words.

'That should be ready in about forty minutes. If you don't mind I'll use the time to have a quick shower, and then…'

The words dried on his lips as he turned to see her moving about the small living room, occasionally stopping to examine something more closely. As he spoke she had come to a halt in front of the old oak dresser which took up almost all of the length of one wall.

He knew exactly what she had seen, and privately cursed his stupidity in not moving it earlier when he had the chance.

In silence he watched as she reached out and picked up the framed photograph, turning it into the light. Sean could picture in his mind just what she was seeing.

Pete. Taken only that summer, here in the garden of the cottage. With his fair hair falling over his face and a wide, infectious grin, it was his brother to a tee. Folding his arms across his chest, Sean could only watch and wait.

For a second or two she studied the portrait, a faint smile curling her own lips as if in response to its subject's laughing expression. But then she turned, and his heart seemed to slam hard against the walls of his chest as he anticipated the inevitable explosion.

He had thought that he knew exactly what she was going to say. He could almost hear her words inside his head already, and so he was unprepared for what actually happened until it rocked his sense of reality.

'He looks nice,' she said quietly. 'Who is he?'

CHAPTER FIVE

'WHO is he?'

Just three simple words. A polite question, no more. And yet, Leah told herself, anyone would have thought it had been something much more dangerous, terribly ominous. Watching Sean's expression change, she knew she had never seen someone react so violently to something she had thought totally innocuous.

His face was suddenly white with tension—or anger. She couldn't decide which. His skin was drawn tight over his carved cheekbones, making the livid scar stand out in harsh relief against his pallor, and those vivid blue eyes seemed to blaze with cold fire.

'Who *is* he?' he echoed, as if doubting the accuracy of his own hearing. 'What sort of question is that?'

'It was just a polite enquiry! I was interested!'

For a second the words seemed to come from miles away, heard as if through a cloud. But when her muzzy thoughts cleared again a new realisation hit home. There was another, very different possible interpretation of his words.

'Oh, I'm sorry! You don't want me prying into your life.'

Another very different expression told her that she was still on the wrong track.

'Then what...?'

'You know! Why the hell do you ask when you know only too well who he is?'

'But I don't!'

Leah had to struggle against an urge to put her hand to her head to support it. She felt as if her brain was clogged with a mixture of porridge and damp cotton wool, not a combination that made clear thinking at all easy.

She shouldn't have had that glass of wine. It had obviously not agreed with her when combined with exhaustion and the after-effects of shock. She had the beginnings of a headache too, gathering ominously like storm clouds on the horizon.

'I wouldn't have asked if I'd known! Is he—?' He couldn't be, could he? 'He's not your partner?'

'Don't be ridiculous!' The force of his retort would have convinced her even if she had really harboured any doubts. 'You at least should know that I'm not gay!'

Which of course she did know. Only too well.

'Then who...?'

Looking back at the photograph, she noticed one or two things she hadn't spotted at first.

'Is he your brother?'

A surprisingly grim nod was Sean's response, but then his finely shaped mouth curved sardonically.

'And are you going to claim that that was just a lucky guess?'

'What else would it be when I've never seen him before in my life? But if you must know, there was nothing lucky about it. The difference in colouring threw me for a minute, but he's got your eyes, the same mouth...'

But these blue eyes were warm, alight with laughter. They weren't cold and hard, as if formed from the ice that had crystallised on the window panes. The lips, unlike the grim slash of a mouth that spoke so eloquently of Sean's dark mood, were stretched in a wide grin of delight.

At this moment Leah couldn't help wishing that it had been the other, obviously younger brother who had come to her rescue in the dark, snow-filled lane.

'Never?'

It had an odd intonation, one she found it impossible to interpret. But the next moment his expression had changed, becoming one of scathing contempt.

'Come off it, Annie!' he scorned. 'That trick won't work.'

'What trick? And just who is this Annie?'

Suddenly something struck her, bringing her head up sharply. A memory hazed by shock and the events that had overtaken her since then. A question she had meant to ask him when he had first come to her beside her car. Was it really only a few hours ago?

'And while I'm asking the questions, just how *did* you know my surname?'

'Elliot?' His voice had more conviction now, that odd moment of uncertainty having vanished. 'Isn't it obvious? Pete told me, of course.'

'Nothing about this is obvious to me at all! For one thing, Pete—I take it *this* is Pete?'

She waved the photograph in the air, directly under his nose.

Another grim-faced nod was his only response.

'Well, then, *Pete* couldn't have told you a damn thing about me because he wouldn't know me from Adam—or Eve, for that matter. We've never even met, not once! At least, not to my knowledge. And if, just supposing, he has seen me somewhere, then he got my name wrong. Because I'm not *Annie* Elliot, or Annie anything—'

A sudden thought struck, making her break off sharply.

'Oh, Lord! He's not *Annie's* Pete, is he?'

Sean's glare in response to her question felt as if it might have the power to shrivel her into ashes where she stood.

'Of course he's Annie's Pete—*your* Pete. As you—'

'No, my cousin Annie!' Leah inserted sharply. 'She's engaged to a Peter...'

'Oh, very clever!' Sean scorned. 'You're a quick thinker, I'll grant you that. But you're forgetting that you've already responded to the name Elliot.'

'Of course I have. Annie's father and my dad were brothers—well, half-brothers to be exact. Dad's mother was my grandfather's first wife; Uncle Joe's was the second and very much younger one. My surname is Elliot, true, but I was christened Leah—Leah Jane!'

'What sort of game is this?'

He hadn't raised his voice, but the question had the sort

of deadly intensity that was more frightening than if he had actually shouted.

'No game!'

Leah couldn't match his control, and immediately regretted the sharpness of her tone—not least because of the way it made him draw his dark brows together ominously. But she was also disturbed to find that her reply hurt her head, which was beginning to ache quite dreadfully.

'Believe me, I'm not *playing* at anything!' she went on more carefully, adjusting the volume downwards. 'And I can prove that quite simply. Wait here!'

Not giving him a chance to argue further, she marched out of the room and back up the stairs to the bedroom he had allocated to her. Snatching up her handbag from where it lay on the bed, she hurried back, rummaging inside it as she went.

'Right, this should clear things up!'

He didn't appear to have moved, seeming to be standing in exactly the same position as before. But he had obviously drained his wine. The empty glass now stood on the dresser beside the photograph of his brother.

There was a new tautness about the long, powerful body, a strange tension, as if he suddenly anticipated something that he knew he wasn't going to like at all. His eyes had darkened almost to indigo with suspicion as he looked down at the driving licence she thrust under his nose.

'Leah Jane Elliot—see! Or, if you want further evidence, here's my chequebook—credit cards! So now what do you say?'

Nothing. He said nothing at all, but simply stared at the items she had forced into his hands as if they were some deadly poisonous snake about to strike.

At long last he drew a deep, uneven breath and raked one hand roughly through his hair.

'I think perhaps we'd better start again. I seem to have made something of a mistake.'

'The understatement of the year!' Leah retorted, retrieving her property and stuffing it back in her bag. The concession seemed to have been dragged from him. 'Just who did you think I was? *Is* my cousin your brother's fiancée?'

'Ex-fiancée, seeing as she just walked out on him. You didn't know that?' he questioned, when Leah's expressive face showed surprise and confusion.

'I had no idea. But then Annie and I aren't very close, never have been. Our fathers couldn't be more unalike— the proverbial chalk and cheese. As a result they don't see much of each other.'

The mention of her father brought to mind her mother, sitting alone at home. She could only be grateful that she had not paused on her drive north to let the older woman know she planned on arriving early. At least this way her mother would be spared the worry caused by her non-arrival.

'I only heard Annie was engaged last week, and then only because I had to phone her about the car.'

A sudden change in Sean's expression alerted her to the fact that she had just said something that disturbed him.

'The Renault was Annie's car until last week. I bought it off her and her brother drove it down to London for me. Has that got something to do with all this?'

'You could say that! Look, why don't we sit down? This could take some explaining, so we might as well do it in comfort.'

'Comfort' wasn't exactly the sort of feeling she associated with being with Sean Gallagher, Leah reflected wryly. Simply being in the same room as him made her feel as if she was suffering from a permanent electric shock, both physically and mentally.

But she would be glad to sit down. Her legs, already shaky from the after-effects of the accident, now seemed close to total collapse. Probably the dash upstairs had just been the last straw. Her head ached abominably too, making thinking clearly decidedly difficult. With a faint sigh she sank into one of the fireside chairs.

'More wine?' Sean asked. 'You look as if you could do with it,' he persisted when she shook her head.

'What I could "do with" is the explanation you promised.'

Any more alcohol would only aggravate the already
cloudy feeling in her head, and she needed to keep as clear
a mind as possible for what was to come. The situation
since their arrival in the cottage had been difficult enough
to start with. Now it seemed to have become even more
complicated than ever.

'All right.'

Sean had refilled his own glass, and now he moved to
sit opposite her on the other side of the fire.

'As you already know, Pete is my brother—my younger
brother. At twenty-five, he's nine years younger than me.
About three months ago he met a girl at a party.'

'Annie?' Leah interjected, when he paused, staring down
into his wine as if seeking inspiration in its burgundy
depths.

A slow, distracted nod was Sean's response. 'Your
cousin Annie. My brother is a true romantic. He took one
look at her and fell head over heels in love. And apparently
she did too.'

'You don't sound as if you believe either of them,' Leah
put in, reacting to the deep cynicism of his tone.

'I don't,' he returned bluntly. 'Love at first sight—at any
sight—is just a myth—a fantasy for purple-prosed novelists
or adolescents with stars in their eyes and too many hor-
mones throbbing in their bodies. It's not for mature, rational
adults.'

'Amongst whose number you obviously count yourself.'

That earned her a swift, narrow-eyed glare, the frown
that drew those dark, straight brows together obviously in
response to the deliberately satirical emphasis she'd placed
on her words.

'Are you telling me that you don't agree?' he questioned,
his expression and the searing contempt in his tone making
her heart lurch uncomfortably.

'I'm saying that it's never happened to me, but until it
does I'll reserve judgement.'

'So you don't love this fiancé of yours? I take it there *is* a genuine fiancé?'

'Of course there is! And of course I love him!'

Was it only in her own ears that her voice sounded too shrill, too nervously emphatic? Did it reveal the guilty conscience that reminded her of the fact that she hadn't even spared a thought for Andy until it was too late?

And she hadn't been strictly truthful in claiming him as her fiancé. He had asked her to marry him, true, but she hadn't said yes. Instead she had asked for time to think.

The engagement she had used as a defence earlier, when things had gone too far, too fast, didn't actually exist. It had only been called on in a moment of desperation. But she didn't want Sean to know that. It was probably much safer for him to continue to believe she was committed to someone else.

'But we're not talking about me. I'm still waiting to know why you should believe I was your brother's fiancée. I take it something went wrong with this magical relationship?'

Sean inclined his dark head in agreement.

'Not at first. Then it was all sweetness and light. But then—things happened that meant Pete couldn't put their relationship first for a while. It seemed he was lucky. Annie was prepared to wait until his time was his own again, and from then on they were like love's young dream. Within a week they were engaged and the wedding was to have been in the New Year—they said they couldn't bear to wait any longer. But today he rang up in one hell of a state.'

'She'd broken it off?'

Leah felt saddened by the thought that the story had an unhappy ending. Annie had sounded so full of things when she had spoken to her the week before, and she would have liked her cousin and her fiancé to prove that true love *did* exist, if only to spite Pete's cynical older brother.

Again Sean nodded. 'She said there was someone else. Gave him back his ring and just walked out.'

Leah frowned. 'That doesn't sound like Annie.'

'It's what happened.' Sean shrugged off her interjection.
'Pete was in a real state about it. It hit him very hard.'

'So how did you get involved in all this?'

'Annie was driving home for Christmas. She would have
had to pass through Appleton on her way and she usually
called in at the Night Owl Café *en route*. I was supposed
to try to talk to her, or at least hold onto her until Pete
could get here. Instead I found you.'

'But didn't you know...?' Leah's voice was constricted.
She was thinking back over the events of the evening, piec-
ing them together in her mind.

'That you weren't Annie? How could I? I've never actually met the woman. All I knew was that I was looking
for a gorgeous long-haired brunette in a silver Renault. So
when I found precisely that, naturally I assumed you were
her.'

'Naturally,' Leah echoed sardonically, refusing to let that
'gorgeous long-haired brunette' register in her thoughts. It
would only distract her far too much if she did. 'It strikes
me that you've made rather too many assumptions all
along.'

Sean's head came up sharply, a dark frown settling on
his handsome features at her critical tone.

'Well, what odds would *you* have given for there being
two dark-haired women, with the same surname, driving
the same car?'

'True,' Leah was forced to admit. 'And it is Annie's
car—or was.'

He had called her Miss Elliot, and, dazed and in shock,
she hadn't asked how he'd known her name, she acknowledged. Perhaps if she had then it might not have come to
this. It was impossible not to wonder how different things
might have been if his brother had never phoned him, and
Sean had come across her simply as some complete
stranger, not thinking she was Annie.

'Annie only offered me the Renault because she'd got a
new job with a company car,' she said slowly. 'If she
hadn't, I'd have been in my old blue Mini.'

And, if she had, then how would that have changed things? The question wasn't an easy one to contemplate. She didn't even know how she wanted it to have been.

'I'm not really used to it yet. I suppose that's why the accident happened.'

'That, and the most atrocious driving conditions for a decade,' Sean put in drily.

'You're right about that.'

Leah shivered at the memory, then found that the cold, creeping sensation wouldn't leave her. Edging her chair a little closer to the fire, she held out her hands to the blaze and was shocked to find that they were shaking quite badly. Her head hurt so much that it was an effort to think clearly.

'You must care a lot for your brother if you were prepared to go out in such weather.'

'I do,' Sean declared abruptly. 'His happiness means a lot to me. He was there when I needed him, so it was the least I could do.'

'So much that you'd risk your...' The words faded as she realised the truth. 'Your accident! That was it, wasn't it? I mean, that was why Pete and Annie couldn't be together at first. He was looking after you!'

'You're very perceptive.'

The words themselves had no bite, but the way he snapped them out, the far from complimentary intonation, warned her that this wasn't a subject he was prepared to let her pry into further.

'So, even though you don't believe in love, you were prepared to go out into a blizzard, kidnap Annie and bring her back.'

It was crazy that it mattered, foolish to feel the lift of her heart at the thought that he could at least do that.

'Not kidnap,' Sean reproved. 'After all, you came willingly enough.'

And she had had cause to wonder on more than one occasion just how stupid she had been to do so. But she had needed help, and she wasn't the wayward fiancée he had believed her to be. It was impossible not to speculate what might have happened if she *had* been Annie Elliot.

Would that passionate encounter still have taken place then? Or was she simply chasing rainbows to believe that Sean's response had been for *her* alone? Wasn't it possible that, working in the world of acting, with its notoriously fickle approach to relationships, he was perfectly capable of making up to any presentable woman he met?

Just recalling the emotions and physical sensations that had overwhelmed her in those few brief minutes made Leah's body temperature swing from icy cold to boiling hot in the space of a heartbeat. Suddenly desperately uncomfortable, she shifted awkwardly in her seat, edging away from the fire she had sought so eagerly just moments before.

'But you didn't say you were Pete's brother, which...'

'I've explained that Annie and I have never met. And Pete hasn't told her that he's related to *the* Sean Gallagher. He knows how much I want to keep my family life private, so he was waiting until I went up there for the New Year before he let on.'

'But you were prepared to go public if it meant getting her to come back here with you? Tell me, did you reckon on that as your ace card? If Annie had refused to come for Pete's sake, then did you think that the thought of being alone with *"the"* Sean Gallagher...'

Deliberately she echoed his own phrase, adding an extra edge of sarcasm to the words.

'Would that have been a carrot you could dangle in front of her nose? Are you so arrogant as to believe that no woman could resist the chance to be with TV's hunk of the year?'

The scathing look he turned on her seared such contempt over the length of her body that she almost expected her clothes to scorch in its wake. It was then that the memory of the way she had been prepared to let him believe precisely that about her own behaviour returned to haunt her, adding another painful twist to her already hopelessly tangled feelings.

But Sean didn't deign to honour her question with an answer.

'I told you—Pete could ask anything of me.' It was a simple, emotionless statement, and one she found herself believing implicitly.

'But now you won't have to.'

'No,' he conceded. 'Now I won't have to. Unless, of course, you decide to take the story to the press.'

Indignation had her sitting up straighter in her chair, her eyes flashing defiance.

'What sort of a louse do you think I am? I don't even *read* the scandal press, let alone supply them with sordid tittle-tattle for their copy!'

'It would make a great exclusive— "TV Hunk Kidnapped Me and Took Me to Hideaway Love-Nest".' His mouth curled around the words in evident distaste. 'They'd pay pretty well.'

This was even worse. Leah bridled at just the thought.

'I don't need any money! I have a good job that pays a pretty decent salary.'

'Doing what?'

'I'm the manageress of a travel agency in Wimbledon, if you must know. So you see, I wouldn't need any hand-outs.'

'Everyone could do with a little bit more money.'

It was tossed at her over his shoulder as he got up to refill his glass. But then he seemed to lose interest abruptly, putting it down again and flexing his broad shoulders tiredly.

'If I don't have that shower now there won't be time before the meal's ready.'

His casual disregard of her righteous indignation riled Leah further.

'We haven't finished talking!'

Half-turned towards the door, Sean froze at her tone.

Slowly he swung back again, looking down at her with a look in his eyes that turned her blood to ice.

'I have,' he declared curtly. 'I've explained—'

'You've *explained*!' Leah echoed bitterly. 'The bare facts—that's it!'

'What else is needed?' It sounded almost weary, like a father whose patience has been overstretched by explaining matters to a stubborn child.

'Quite a lot, really. An apology, for one!'

'An apology? For what?'

Suddenly Leah wished desperately that she wasn't sitting down. His size and strength were awesome enough when she could look him in the face; from her current position he seemed to tower over her unnervingly. But a worrying sense of uncertainty about whether her legs would actually support her kept her unwillingly in her seat as she responded.

'For the way you treated me. For bringing me here under false pretences—for…'

The words shrivelled on her lips as she saw in his face the changes she was already beginning to recognise as danger signs: the narrowed eyes, the drawing together of those dark brows.

'An apology,' he repeated in an ominously different way, one that made her shiver as if a finger as cold as the snow outside had trailed down her spine. 'Let's see—I apologise for mistaking you for someone else. But even you admitted that that was a coincidence no one could have foreseen.'

'I—'

Leah opened her mouth to protest but he ignored her, continuing in a coldly controlled way that made all the tiny hairs on her skin lift in fearful response.

'But should I apologise for bringing you here when to leave you would have meant abandoning you to a very cold, uncomfortable and possibly dangerous night stranded in your car? Should I be sorry that I offered you a roof over your head for the night, together with warmth, food…?'

'For trying to seduce me!'

There, it was out. But Sean's reaction was not at all what she had anticipated. His short, harsh bark of laughter brought her gaze to his face in a rush, seeing the glitter of cynical amusement in the denim-blue of his eyes, the smile that was a travesty of any real expression of humour.

'For *seducing* you?' he echoed, emphasising the word sardonically. 'Oh, no, my darling Leah, I don't apologise for anything that felt so right, so necessary. And, to be perfectly accurate, I didn't try to seduce you. If anything it was mutual; we seduced each other. You were a willing partner in all this, and I'm certainly not sorry about any of it. As a matter of fact, I would very much like to try it again some time.'

As he spoke he took a step towards her, that smile growing wider as she glared at him furiously.

'Oh, no, you don't!' she flung up at him, refusing to let him see how the way he towered over her made her feel small and weak—not a sensation she was used to at all. 'It'll be a cold day in hell before I let you touch me again!'

She expected anger, nerved herself to face the onslaught of his black fury, but to her surprise it didn't come. Instead, she was subjected to another of those hard, humourless laughs as his eyes raked over her, from her shining dark head to her small bare toes as they curled on the rug.

'Is that a fact?' he drawled lazily. 'Well, in that case I'd better make sure that I have a very cold shower instead of the hot one I had planned on. Are you sure I can't persuade you to join me?'

Leah didn't deign to honour his question with an answer, turning her head away mutinously rather than meet the cruel mockery in his eyes. Another of those hateful laughs had her gritting her teeth against an unthinking and potentially dangerous response, her slim body held as taut as a bowstring until she heard him leave the room.

As the door closed behind him she relaxed at last, letting go of the breath she had been holding in and slumping weakly back against the cushions. She was breathing fast

and shallow, her heart racing inside a chest that felt raw
and tight, and now it wasn't just her head but her whole
body that ached.

What was she going to do? She couldn't stay here. The
prospect of sharing such a confined space with a man like
Sean was enough to bring her out in a cold sweat just thinking about it.

In a rush of panic she thrust her feet into her dilapidated
shoes and stood up, snatching up her bag and heading for
the hall. Her mind full of thoughts of escape, she flung open
the front door and then stopped dead, a moan of defeat
escaping her.

'Oh, no!'

The scene that met her eyes killed all hope as effectively
as if it had been buried under the frozen blanket that covered everything for miles.

Snow. Inches deep. It was all that she could see to the
right or left, smooth and impassable, heavy drifts having
blown across what had been the road up to the cottage.
Even the car, parked only so very recently, was buried under a thick coating of the stuff, and it was clearly not going
to move again in the near future.

She would be risking life and limb if she was foolish
enough to try venturing out, even if she had any idea of
which direction to take. But every landmark, every clue to
the way back to her car or the nearest village had been
obliterated by the thick white coating. It was like some
space landscape, alien and dangerous.

And quite honestly she didn't feel well enough to try.
Miserably she recalled the way almost the entire staff of
the travel agency had gone down with a vicious virus at
some point over the previous couple of weeks. Only that
morning Melanie had joked that it would be Leah's turn
next.

'Oh, please, no!' she prayed now. 'I've enough to cope
with, without that as well.'

She had no option but to stay put. With a despondent
sigh Leah closed the door again.

The chill from outside seemed to have invaded right to her bones, and she hurried into the living room, huddling close to the fire once more in a vain attempt to get warm. From upstairs she could hear the sounds of the rush of water in the shower and Sean's movements in the bathroom.

Sean. Who was he? What was he? Oh, she knew all the superficial things, like how old he was, what he did for a living. Anyone who watched television had to be aware of that. But what did she really know about the man she was now trapped with, forced to share this small cottage with for God knew how long?

She had felt so happy, so relieved when he had first appeared. Then he had seemed like a knight in shining armour, coming to her rescue at just the right moment. And the fact that his face was familiar, if only from her TV screen, had added to that unreal feeling, knocking her off balance emotionally.

'Off balance indeed!' she muttered aloud. 'You said it, girl!'

So off balance that she had behaved in a way that was totally at odds with the person she had believed herself to be. A way that had clearly given Sean quite the wrong impression of her from the start, just as his role as rescuer had distorted her own judgement badly. That and the fact that he was the most devastatingly attractive man she had ever met.

Face it, kid; he knocked you for six.

Six! More like a dozen, if she admitted to the truth. Her heart twisted on a pang of distress as she admitted that her feelings had been based only on deceptive appearances combined with her own naivety.

What was it Sean had said?

Don't confuse the fictional character he played with reality?

But stupidly, crazily, she had done just that. And the worst of it was that even now she hadn't faced the full truth. He was even more shallow, even more arrogantly selfish than she had let herself think.

Because wasn't it true that even when he had believed that she was Annie, that she was engaged—to his *brother*, for Heaven's sake!—he had still come on to her, and would have made love to her right there and then if she hadn't put a stop to it.

And then he had had the nerve to blame *her* for what had happened!

Upstairs, the sound of the shower had been shut off. Heavy footsteps crossing from the bathroom to the bedroom brought Leah up sharp, reminding her that in a very few minutes Sean would be coming back down and she had no idea how she was going to behave towards him.

It was foolish, it was downright pathetic, but she couldn't hold back a sharp pang of regret for the loss of the knight errant she had believed had come to her rescue. In his place she now had to put—what?

A man who had come to her rescue only because he'd believed she was his brother's fiancée. A man who had been prepared to do anything at all to get that fiancée into his house and keep her there.

A man who, once she was in the house, had not been able to resist attempting to seduce her. A sexual opportunist who, even when he'd found out that she was not who he believed her to be, hadn't shown even the tiniest trace of conscience over the way he had treated her.

'You were a willing partner in all this...' Sean's voice echoed inside her head. 'If anything it was mutual; we seduced each other.'

Oh, God!

With a groan of despair Leah buried her face in her hands, knowing it was impossible to dodge the truth. Since the moment of the crash she hadn't even recognised herself in the way she had behaved.

She had become some other, alien person, a wild, sensual wanton who had responded to Sean in a way that went against all her previously held—securely held, she would have asserted—beliefs about morality, self-preservation and basic common sense. She didn't know how it had happened, but it seemed that Sean Gallagher had the power to strip away the woman she'd believed she was and reveal another, very different person in her place.

And the worst problem was that she no longer knew which of those characters was the *real* Leah. She only knew that with her calmer, more rational self back in control the prospect of revealing the other side ever again was one that made her nerves twist in panic. She didn't dare to contemplate the possible consequences if that Leah got free again—which was a distinct possibility as long as she stayed in this house with this man.

But she had no alternative. She had to stay; there was no way out.

Which was a thought guaranteed to tie her stomach into tight, painful knots as she heard footsteps descending the stairs. Drawing a deep breath, she nerved herself to face Sean once again.

CHAPTER SIX

'YOU haven't eaten very much.'

'I'm not hungry.'

Major understatement, Sean told himself. In spite of her enthusiasm earlier, she'd hardly eaten a damn thing, just picked at her food as if she suspected him of having poisoned it.

In fact, on a couple of occasions since he'd come back into the room, he'd seen her looking at him as if *he* was the poisonous one, some sort of deadly snake about to strike. It wasn't a situation he was used to, and he didn't like being made to feel like an intruder in his own home.

'You can relax, you know.' He saw her wince as the deliberate sarcasm caught her on the raw. 'I'm not about to pounce on you.'

The look she turned on him was frankly sceptical.

'I thought that was precisely what you had in mind.'

'I—'

About to launch into a furious attack, Sean suddenly thought the better of it and closed his mouth with a distinct snap. Like it or not, he had to spend time with this woman until the snow cleared. They could at least try to be civilised.

'I never "pounce",' he declared tautly. 'And believe me, I've never forced a woman yet. I don't intend to start with you.'

He wouldn't have to *force*, an insidious little voice whispered at the back of his mind. All he had to do was to take her in his arms, press his mouth to her warm, sensual lips, kiss her until she made that soft little sound of surrender...

Hell and damnation! What *was* he doing?

Looking across the table, he saw that those amazing eyes

had widened at his muttered imprecation, almost as if she knew just what had been going through his mind.

Suddenly it was impossible to sit opposite her any longer without touching her in some way. Pushing back his chair with a violent movement, he stood up hastily and reached for her half-empty plate, banging it down on top of his own.

'I'll clear these away, then. I take it you don't want anything else?' he added over his shoulder on the way to the kitchen.

'Not for me, thanks.' Her voice was strangely distant. 'But don't let that stop you. You go ahead.'

'I never eat puddings. My mother always said I was born without a sweet tooth. Coffee, then?'

Dumping the plates on the draining board, he swung back to see her getting to her feet.

'That would be nice. Can I help—?'

'No!'

It came out too sharply because his nerves were still tingling from the sensations that had coursed through them only seconds before. He had had to suppress those feelings so violently that he felt raw from the effort.

He couldn't watch as she came into the kitchen, moving swiftly to switch on the kettle.

'I was brought up never to let a guest do anything in the house.'

'And *my* parents taught me always to offer to help,' she said, with a smile that threatened his already shaky grip on his composure. 'Besides, I don't really think that I could call myself a "guest".'

'So how would you describe your situation?'

He had meant his growled 'guest' to be off-putting, and so was thoroughly disconcerted when, having glanced towards the window where the snow flurries were still beating against the glass, she turned back with another of those gut-wrenching smiles.

'Right now I feel like the man in the Bible story who had been left by the side of the road and no one would help him until the Good Samaritan came by.'

'You make it sound as if I'm a candidate for sainthood! And you're forgetting that I picked you up because I thought you were Pete's fiancée.'

The kettle boiled as he spoke, and, grateful for the interruption, he snatched it up. Hastily pouring it into the waiting cafetière, he looked round for the lid which he had discarded somewhere.

'Is this what you want?'

Leah picked up the missing lid from the worktop and handed it to him.

'So are you saying that if you hadn't thought I was Annie, if you'd known I was someone else entirely, you wouldn't have offered to help me?'

'Don't be stupid! What sort of a brute do you think I am? I wouldn't have left a dog out in that blizzard, let alone a woman—any woman.'

Even Marnie? The question slid into his mind while his guard was down.

Yes, damn it, even Marnie! After all, hadn't that been the problem from the start? He'd given her a second chance, believed in her lies, her smiling declarations of understanding, and look where that had got him.

'I'm sorry.'

There was a new note in her voice now, a sudden quaver that made him wonder whether she had somehow picked up on his innermost thoughts, if he had let them show without meaning to.

'Look, couldn't we start again? Act as if we'd only just met, as if we were complete strangers?'

A touch of urgency mixed with—what? Hope?—lit in her eyes.

'As if nothing's happened.'

But something *had* happened, something Sean knew he could never forget. And he damn well didn't *want* to forget it either.

'You ask for a lot, lady,' he began gruffly. But the way the light in those pansy eyes dimmed at his tone caught on something raw, deep inside him, and he hastily adjusted his attitude.

Dumping the cafetière on a tray already laid with cups and a milk jug, he picked it up with an uncharacteristically jerky movement.

'Complete strangers it is.'

Shouldering the door open again, he led the way back into the sitting room, where the fire now blazed so brightly that he didn't bother to switch on the lights, leaving it instead in half-shadow.

'So, Miss Elliot...'

Busy pouring the coffee, he noted how, like him, she avoided the settee, choosing instead to sit in the chair opposite his, so that they faced each other across the fireside rug. She didn't relax back into it, but sat stiffly on the edge of the cushion, her back upright, knees primly together.

'Tell me about yourself. Like—how you want your coffee, for a start.'

'Just milk, please, no sugar.'

She tried to follow his lead, but there was an unevenness in her words that betrayed the effort she was making, and when he handed her the cup her face looked pale and tense in the flickering firelight.

'What do you want to know?' she added as he seated himself again.

'A bit more about what you do would be a good place to start.' Years of training and acting experience kept his voice smoothly controlled. 'After all, you have the advantage of me there.'

'Doesn't it bother you to have your life such public property?'

The question escaped her with a spontaneity that changed her appearance dramatically. The restraint that had held her shapely body taut and her face frozen eased suddenly, making her look younger, warmer, disturbingly vulnerable.

'I mean, I'd hate it if every detail of what I did was a subject of gossip and comment for everyone and anyone.' She actually shuddered at the thought.

'It comes with the job; I knew that when I started out. You learn to live with it. But I have to admit that sometimes I just want to tell everyone to go to hell and leave me alone.'

'Like now, when you're convalescing from an accident? I can see why you'd want to be here, in this cottage, instead of somewhere much more public. It's quiet and private, and you can stay here until you're ready to face the world again. Is that why you hadn't met your brother's fiancée—because you wanted to keep your identity private?'

'Precisely.'

So she was smart as well as beautiful. It was a potentially dangerous combination. An intriguing one too, making him want to know much more about her.

'But we were talking about you. I want to know all about your high-flying career in the travel industry.' He didn't trouble to hide the genuine interest in his voice, and knew from her face that she had noted it too, and been surprised by it.

'It's hardly high-flying. I work in a branch of a major national travel agent's. I started as a trainee straight from school and worked my way up. I was made manageress just three months ago.'

'Pretty good going for someone of—what—twenty-two?'

A tiny smile flickered over her lips. 'Twenty-five, actually. And if you're trying to flatter me...'

'Flattery didn't come into it. I was simply trying to guess how old you are. Not that accurate a guess, I admit, but then I'm better with foot sizes than I am with ages.'

'You weren't that far—*Foot sizes*?'

The look she turned on him over her coffee cup was full of amused disbelief, her eyes lighting with a new warmth.

'That's right.' Sean found himself smiling in response to her confusion. 'I have vast experience of women's feet.'

Curiosity getting the better of her, she slipped her foot out of her shoe and lifted it towards him, wriggling her toes almost flirtatiously.

'Five and a half,' Sean declared confidently, and knew

he was right by the way her head went back, her eyes widening in amazement.

'But how…?'

Laughing aloud, he decided to put her out of her misery.

'I wasn't always a household name. I've done my share of "resting" between acting jobs, sometimes for far longer than I care to recall. On those occasions I took any job that was offered, which is how I came to spend almost a year working in a shoe shop.'

'You!' Her delighted splutter of laughter told him how incongruous she found the idea. 'I'll bet you were a dynamite salesman. All you'd have to do is to turn on that famous charm of yours and any woman would buy anything you offered her.'

'Now who's using flattery?'

This was better; she'd relaxed a lot. That smile had wiped some of the pinched look from her face, though she was still pale.

'So tell me about work in the travel agency. Do you get to visit the places you offer to people for holidays?'

'Sometimes. It's one of the perks of the job. And it helps to be able to talk about resorts if we've actually been there.'

'And where would *you* go on holiday? What country really attracts you? Or is that like asking a chef what food he eats? When you're working with it all the time, do you lose interest?'

'Oh, no! I love to travel. For a while I considered being a courier rather than work at the agency, but I decided I'd rather see places on a holiday than work there. Where do I like best? That's difficult.'

Her brows came together into a thoughtful frown as she considered.

'I love Spain—especially Almería in the south—and Granada's quite wonderful. And I'd like to see more of Canada; I've only been to Toronto. But the place I love best in the whole world—so far—has to be Madeira.'

Her face was alight with enthusiasm now, and she had

kicked off the other shoe, curling her legs up under her in the chair.

She looked like a small child, Sean thought, his heart thudding suddenly as her smile sparked off thoughts that were definitely not appropriate to the age she appeared to be. He had to drag his gaze from her glowing eyes, the smiling mouth, refusing to allow himself to remember how it had felt to have it soften under his own.

'I have this thing about islands,' Leah continued, oblivious to his sudden silence. 'And Madeira has to be one of the loveliest I've ever visited. The flowers are amazing, even at the sides of the roads. And they have this system of irrigation channels—*levadas*—high in the hills that you can walk along.'

'Where the air is scented with eucalyptus leaves,' Sean inserted, purely in order to distract his thoughts, then wishing that he hadn't as his comment drew those violet eyes to his face.

'You've been there?'

Slowly he nodded. 'A couple of years ago, with Pete. Like every tourist, we did the *levada* walks.'

'And of course you had afternoon tea on the terrace at Reids Hotel?'

'Of course!'

What had put that flush of colour in her cheeks? Was it simply the coffee, or the effect of the fire? It looked too hectic for that, making him watch her more closely as her smile faded and she rubbed at her temple, her eyes half closed.

'Are you all right?'

'Mmm.' It was vague, distracted. 'It's just that I can't seem to get warm.'

'But it's almost too hot in here now.'

'Is it?' She sounded surprised. 'I don't think I've really got over being caught in the snow. Perhaps I should have put a thicker jumper on.'

With an obvious effort she focused her gaze on him again.

'Is Pete your only brother, or are there any more of you?'

'Just Pete, and he's very much my kid brother, being so much younger. I've always looked after him, right from our schooldays.'

'And you're still doing it now. Isn't it time you let him handle his own problems?'

'Yeah, well...'

Getting to his feet, Sean moved to pour himself more coffee. When he waved the pot in her direction, one eyebrow lifting enquiringly, Leah shook her head and laid her hand over the top of her cup. But her movement wasn't quick enough to hide the fact that it was still almost full, the drink barely touched.

'He did his share of taking care of me. Is there something wrong with the coffee?'

'Oh, no...'

She stared down at her cup as if only just becoming aware of it.

'It's just that I'm not very thirsty.'

'Like you weren't very hungry.'

'Well, I wasn't! I expect you mean when you had your accident—that was when your brother took care of you?'

Sean recognised a deliberate change of subject when he heard one, but he decided to go along with her for now. As he returned to his chair he studied her face more closely, noting uneasily that her eyes looked over-bright and her hands were tightly clenched together in her lap.

'Yes, Pete was my support after the accident. He dropped everything, left his business in the hands of his deputy, and came to stay with me for as long as he was needed. He'd still be here now if I'd let him, but I decided he'd done enough and his fiancée needed him more than I did.'

When the memory of his brother's frantic phone call today came into his mind he gave a snort of cynical laughter.

'Perhaps I'd have done better to keep him with me. If he'd never gone back to her then she wouldn't have been able to hurt him as she has done.'

'I doubt if Pete would see it that way,' Leah put in quietly. 'From what you told me, he obviously still loves Annie and wants her back.'

'More fool him.' The cynicism was deeper now, harsh and dark as pitch. 'If you ask me, love's an overrated emotion. It causes more trouble than it's worth.'

'Oh, but you can't mean that!'

'Can't I?'

In his thoughts, the echoes of Marnie's voice saying 'But, Sean, I *love* you!' gave an added edge to the sardonic question.

'In my experience, that's exactly how it is.'

'But surely your parents...'

'My father didn't stay around long enough to get to know that he'd sired a second son. That's why Pete and I are so close. I was the only male role model in his life.'

'But you were only a child yourself!'

Her obvious concern, the shadows in her eyes, made him suddenly uncomfortable enough with the intimacy of the firelit room to get out of his chair and move to snap on the lights.

'I was old enough to realise that "I love you" rarely means for ever.'

Blinking in the sudden brightness, Leah looked paler than ever, her face drawn as she put her cup down on the tiled hearth, obviously abandoning her half-hearted attempt to drink the coffee.

She didn't look well. Sean frowned in concern. Was it shock, or something more?

'I don't agree...'

'But of course—I don't expect that you would. You couldn't, or you would never have agreed to marry what's-his-name.'

'Andy.' Her voice was low and slightly shaken, and she lifted a hand to her eyes as if to hide their expression from him.

'Yeah—Andy.' He repeated the name savagely. The rush of bitterness was so strong that he could almost taste it, burning in his mouth.

For all too short a time he had actually forgotten.
Forgotten about this Andy.

He had been so relieved that she wasn't engaged to his
brother that he'd forgotten that she still had a fiancé in the
wings somewhere. In the space of those few brief minutes
he had found himself lulled into a false sense of ease.
Dammit, he had even come close to *liking* her!

'Do you want to know about Andy?'

She had taken her hands down now, and had turned to
face him. Her eyes were disturbing dark pools over the
pallor of her cheeks. But he wouldn't let himself consider
his earlier concern. It would make him too vulnerable to
her, something that was dangerously threatening to his self-
control.

'Shall I tell you…?'

'No! I don't want to know anything about him!'

He didn't want to learn any details. Didn't want to see
her face change as she talked of the man she was to marry.
Her eyes would glow, her mouth soften, curling into a smile
as she said the name of the man she loved.

Hell, no! Not *loved*! How could she claim to love this
Andy and then act as she had done? How could she promise
to marry one man, forsaking all others, in the words of the
wedding service, and then be so wild and wantonly willing
in his arms?

'But you should know—'

The sentence was never completed. What she had been
about to say was abruptly cut off, her tongue freezing at
the shrill sound that echoed throughout the cottage, only
slightly muffled by the barrier of a couple of closed doors.
Seeing the change in her face, Sean could only swear savagely.

'A telephone!' Shock and bewilderment showed in her
eyes, shaded her voice. 'You have a telephone! But you
said…'

'I know,' he began, his words falling into the sudden
silence as, the damage done, his answering-machine responded to the call. 'I…'

But Leah ignored his attempt to explain, getting to her feet in a rush.

'You deceived me!' The violet eyes flashed in fury, but there was something darker, disturbingly raw in their amethyst depths. 'You let me believe I couldn't contact anyone and all the time you were lying!'

'I thought you were Pete's fiancée. I didn't want you contacting the other man he said she'd left him for.'

Her anger was easier to face than the distress of just seconds before. That reproachful look had twisted in his guts so sharply that he still felt the discomfort.

'But you've known I wasn't Annie for well over an hour now, and yet you still—'

The violent gesture she made proved her undoing, seeming to throw her off balance, so that she swayed on her feet, one hand going out to grasp at the back of her chair for support.

'Sean...'

Almost in spite of herself, it seemed, she cried his name, turning a look full of fearful appeal on him, one that wrenched at his emotions again.

'What is it?'

Instinct pushing him into action before he was even capable of thought, he moved forward swiftly, his hands closing over her arms.

Oh, God, no, this was not what he wanted. Or, rather, *yes*, it was exactly what he wanted—but what he had resolved to deny himself. The warmth of her body, the softness of her skin, the sound of her breathing through her partially opened lips all assailed him like a physical blow so that his head reeled with the impact.

The perfume she had worn earlier had been washed away in the shower, to be replaced by a sweet, clean, delicate scent that was hers alone. Just to inhale it twisted nerves deep inside him, making his body respond instantaneously. He had to struggle against the urge to rest his head against hers, feel the soft silkiness of the glossy dark hair against his face.

'Sean...'

She said his name again, this time with an edge of desperation to the word, and he saw the frown that drew her dark brows together.

'Leah? Are you OK?'

His heart kicked painfully in his chest as she slid her arms upwards, linking them around his neck. The movement brought her even closer, the soft swell of her breasts crushed against the wall of his ribcage. Dear God, she must know—must *feel* what she was doing to him!

But then she made a small sound in her throat, like a young child nestling close to a loved parent, and she lifted her face to his, resting the satin of her cheek against his jaw.

Abruptly his mood changed as a slow, creeping sense of unease slid into his mind. It was followed speedily by an unexpected feeling of concern, the conviction that all was not right. And with that came the need to help, to protect, to care for her.

'What is it?' he asked gently.

Dear God, something was very wrong! Her skin was so hot; she was burning up! He touched her face lightly, wincing at what he felt there.

'Leah! What *is* it?'

His hand under her chin lifted her face, and a dark frown drew his brows together as he saw the faraway, glazed look in her eyes.

She opened her mouth, tried to form the words, but failed. Shaking her head in weak disgust at herself, she tried again, but with no more success, her eyes filling with tears of frustration. Then suddenly, with a small, choking cry, she simply crumpled in his arms and collapsed like a delicate autumn leaf, falling softly to the ground.

CHAPTER SEVEN

A TELEPHONE!

The shocked thought was the first thing to go through Leah's mind when she finally struggled up from deep oceans of sleep.

He had a telephone, and all this time he had lied to her, pretending that it didn't exist!

The final, furious realisation jerked her fully awake. Her eyes opened with a snap and she stared up at the cream-painted ceiling above her.

Cream-painted ceiling?

There was something wrong here. Slowly, carefully, she tried to collect her muddled thoughts, striving to focus on just why she felt so uneasy. Her frowning gaze travelled across the ceiling to the top of the window then down over the green curtains and on to the toning carpet of the bedroom Sean had assigned to her.

Bedroom! That was it.

The realisation had her jerking upright, then swiftly lowering her head back onto the pillows as it swam sickeningly, making the room seem to swing round her.

Think!

She hadn't been in the bedroom, but downstairs. Her head had hurt, the ache growing into an unyielding, gnawing pain, and then that terrible feeling of sickness had made things impossible to bear. She had got to her feet and then...

Then it had seemed as if a huge dark wave had swept over her, knocking her off her feet and engulfing her completely.

'Oh, God!'

The words escaped in a weak whisper as she stirred restlessly. Her mood sharpened into a lurching panic as the

movement and the brush of the fine sheets against her skin
brought home to her the disturbing fact that both her jeans
and her jumper had gone. A further frantic exploration with
her fingertips left no room for doubt. Under the covers she
was completely naked.

'So you're awake.'

The voice sounded from behind her, reaction jerking her
round to stare straight into Sean's vivid blue eyes.

'That's progress at least,' he continued. 'I was beginning
to think...'

But Leah wasn't listening.

'What have you done to me?' she flung at him, hearing
the weak quiver in her voice that betrayed her inner turmoil.

'"Done"?' The dark straight brows drew together in a
frown. 'I've done nothing...'

'Nothing!' It was a high-pitched shriek escaping a throat
that seemed dry and tight with fear. 'I haven't a stitch on!
You took my clothes.'

He didn't even look abashed, just shrugged his shoulders
in a gesture that was casually dismissive of her outrage.

'Yeah, well, that was rather necessary.' His eyes met her
indignant violet ones without a trace of embarrassment.
'You wouldn't have been comfortable if I'd left you fully
clothed.'

'Comfortable!' Leah almost choked on the word as she
struggled to get a grip on thoughts that seemed to slip and
slide inside her head like slivers of soap in a bowl of water.

He hadn't been wearing those clothes before, she registered uneasily. The dark green sweatshirt and black cords
were unfamiliar from the meal they had shared. So when
had he changed?

And—Oh, God!—another realisation made her heart
clench in fear. It was not the darkness of the night that
showed between a crack in the curtains but the full light of
day. Immediately a thousand new worries surfaced in her
mind, beating at her thoughts like a multitude of trapped
butterfly wings.

Was it possible? Could he have drugged her? Put something in her drink?

'How dare you—?'

'Calm down, lady.'

Sean had seen the flare of distress in her eyes.

'"Dare" doesn't come into it. And you can forget the dark, perverted sexual feelings you're obviously determined to attribute to me. I acted for your comfort, pure and simple, and nothing else. You fainted; you were out cold—or, rather, not cold at all, but burning up with some sort of fever. Which reminds me.'

At last he moved from his position in the doorway, coming fully into the room to place a glass of water on the bedside table.

'Try and drink some of this; it'll do you good. And, forgive me, but...'

The hand that rested on her forehead was cool and impersonal, his touch so light that she had barely time to register it before he lifted it away again.

'There, that wasn't so bad, was it?' The thread of mockery in the question caught her on the raw. 'You seem much less feverish. How do you feel now?'

'OK.'

Leah's response came warily, and her eyes were still dark with suspicion as she studied him. It all sounded very plausible, but she couldn't rid herself of the thought that had been uppermost in her mind when she had woken. Sean had set out to deliberately deceive her once. Who was to say that he wasn't prepared to do it again?

'I'm a bit wrung out.'

That was an understatement if there ever was one. She felt as if she had just gone ten rounds with a heavyweight champion, her limbs aching and frighteningly weak.

'Not surprising.' Sean nodded soberly. 'You'll feel that way for a while yet, I expect. You've had a nasty couple of days.'

'Days!'

Leah didn't care if she sounded like a dazed parrot, echoing everything he said. The impact of his words hit home so violently that she struggled to sit up, remembering her unclothed state only at the last moment, and hastily pulling the duvet up around her shoulders again.

'Did you say *days*? How long…?'

'You've been ill for three days,' Sean supplied when confusion cut the sentence off unfinished.

He came to sit on the bed, deliberately keeping his distance from her as he perched at the foot of the mattress.

'You had some foul sort of virus. The doctor said—'

'Doctor? What doctor?'

Had someone got through to the cottage while she had been ill? Couldn't he have taken her away with him?

'The one I rang when you passed out on me. I'm not so irresponsible that I'd neglect to get medical advice when you were obviously pretty sick.' The sharpness of his tone told her how much even the thought of her suspicion had stung.

'That wasn't what I meant.'

'Oh, so you were wondering if he'd fought his way through the snow to come to your bedside? Well, I'm sorry to disappoint you, but he did no such thing. He didn't have to. He practically told me all your symptoms without even bothering to ask. It seems half the population's down with this virus. Obviously it was already in your system when you left London, and the crash was just the last straw. You were completely out of it there for a while.'

So it seemed, Leah reflected bemusedly. How could she have lost three days just like that? But now that the feeling that seemed to have clouded her brain like clinging cotton wool was beginning to ease she realised that the passing of time was not such a shock as she had at first believed it to be.

She had vague, disjointed memories of feeling dreadfully ill, times when she seemed to have been burning up, when she had surfaced from the febrile dreams that had gripped her to find her whole body drenched in sweat. There had been other occasions when quite the opposite had happened, when she had shivered and moaned, unable to get warm.

And all that time someone had been there. Someone with gentle hands and a soft, soothing voice. Someone who had bathed her and fed her sips of cooling water when her throat was parched, and who had wrapped her up, providing hot water bottles, when she had suffered from the cold. She even seemed to recall...

But her mind skittered away from a memory that she was sure must just have been the result of the delirium that had accompanied the fever.

'You looked after me all that time?'

'There was no one else here to do it.' Sean's tone was calm and matter-of-fact, his demeanour as impersonal as any doctor's. It was that which gave Leah the courage to ask the next question that burned in her mind.

'And my clothes?'

'Like I said, I thought you'd be more comfortable out of them. I found a nightdress in your case, but at the height of the fever it got soaked so I replaced it with a tee-shirt of mine. I had to do that a couple of times altogether—they're downstairs in the washer right now.'

Her relief must show on her face, Leah knew. She was too weak, too exhausted, to hide the way she was feeling. But still there was one thing that fretted at her thoughts.

'I—wasn't always hot,' she said carefully.

But not carefully enough. That much was clear from the frown that darkened Sean's face, the way his mouth clamped shut, a muscle jerking at the side of his jaw with the effort he was making to hold something back.

'No, there were times when you just couldn't get warm.'

Each word was cold and precise, as if it was formed in letters of ice.

'And, yes...'

Clearly he had anticipated what her next question would be.

'Last night I did the only thing possible to get you warm again. I got in beside you. But, no, whatever your suspicious little mind is thinking, I didn't touch you, or at least no more than I absolutely had to in order to make you comfortable. I'm not the depraved monster you seem to believe I am, and neither am I so desperate for a woman as to force myself on any unconscious female.'

Burning colour that had nothing to do with a possible temperature flooded into Leah's cheeks at his ominously sardonic tone.

'I never thought you were.'

'Oh, yes, you did, sweetheart. It's written all over that lovely face of yours. But, quite frankly, comatose victims just don't turn me on. I prefer my lovers wide awake and actively willing.'

It was only as she flinched away from the bitter humour that Leah realised too late that it had not been there before. Her own foolish fears had sparked off that reaction in Sean, and she had only herself to blame if he turned away from her as he did now. But not before she had seen that the tight-jawed control was back, thinning his generous mouth to a cold, hard line.

'Sean...'

It was just a faint thread of sound, but it was enough to still him as he marched towards the door. She saw how his head moved slightly. Only his head, as he turned a swift, sideways glance in her direction.

But that was all. Apart from that one small movement, every muscle in the long body was taut with ruthlessly controlled anger as he waited, not saying a word.

'I'm sorry. I should have known... And thank you for taking care of me.'

'I could hardly leave you in an unconscious heap on the living room floor.'

There was only the slightest trace of dry humour in his response, but at least it was a start. Then abruptly he seemed to reconsider, and a little of his tension eased as he turned back to her.

'Do you think you could try to eat something now? It

would do you a lot of good. You'll be faint from lack of
food as much as from anything else. Some soup, perhaps?'

'I'd like that, thanks.'

Perhaps she would feel better with something in her
stomach, she reflected as she listened to his footsteps descending the stairs. Some food might ease the fuzzy, light-
headed feeling that made it seem as if she couldn't quite
get a grip on anything.

Left alone, she made herself face up to what had happened, and she found that an uncomfortable stab from her
conscience made her twist uneasily in the bed. She had
been particularly ungracious to Sean, and without much jus-
tification. After all, he had cared for her for three days and
nights, and all she had shown him was suspicion and dis-
trust.

But then the thought that had come to her as she had
woken returned to haunt her, and anger sparked through
her again, pushing away the weaker feelings she had been
prey to.

Before she had time to recover, Sean was back in the
room. He carried a tray, on which was a bowl of the soup
he had promised, and slung over one arm was a pale blue
tee-shirt which he tossed onto the bed.

'Here, this will preserve your modesty until your nightdress is dry again. I had hoped it would be washed and
dried before now, but the power has only just come back
on.'

Reaching for the tee-shirt, Leah froze, intrigued by his
comment.

'The power?'

Sean nodded his dark head. 'The snow must have
brought cables down somewhere. We were without any
electricity for over twenty-four hours. That's why I had to
resort to extreme measures to keep you warm.'

'Oh...'

One glance at the dancing mockery in those blue eyes
had her colouring in confusion. Snatching up the tee-shirt

again, she pulled it over her head, as much to hide her embarrassment as to cover herself.

It was a struggle to get into the simple garment while remaining in bed. The need to keep the quilt pulled up over her nakedness necessitated some awkward wriggling and adjustment, but she was thankful to find that, being wide and loose, the shirt came down well on to her hips. When she finally settled back against the pillows again it was to find Sean regarding her with undisguised amusement.

'Isn't it a little too late for such modesty?' he asked softly, his sensual mouth curling wickedly. 'Surely there's nothing I haven't seen already.'

'I was ill then—unconscious!' Leah returned with some force.

'Actually, I was thinking of another, very different occasion,' Sean drawled back.

His amusement grew as he saw her pause to consider, then do a mental double-take as she realised precisely the occasion he was talking about, on her arrival at the cottage that first evening.

'All the more reason to avoid any possible repetition of such events.'

'You have a beautiful body, darling.'

Sean's voice was silky with implications, just the thought of which raised goosebumps of reaction all over Leah's skin.

'As I'm sure you're only too aware. But it takes more than a glimpse of a naked female form to have me panting with lust. The women I've taken to bed have been more than willing—'

'I'll bet!' Leah muttered darkly, but Sean ignored her sarcastic interjection.

'And I wouldn't want it any other way.'

He waited a nicely calculated moment, just long enough for her tension to subside and a deeper embarrassment to take its place, before he spoke again.

'The willing part will come soon enough. I'm quite prepared to wait.'

'Then you'll wait till hell freezes over!'

She'd been there once before, and her own reaction, the total loss of control she had experienced had shaken her. It was not something she fancied risking again.

Her furious retort brought a wicked grin to Sean's mouth.

'You are feeling better,' he drawled. 'Well, we'll see. Are you ready for your soup now?'

Privately, Leah suspected that any food would stick in her throat, choking her, but spooning it up gave her something to do, an action to concentrate on so that she didn't have to meet those tauntingly brilliant blue eyes. In the end she found it surprisingly easy to swallow, and was grateful for the warmth it brought to her weakened body.

While she ate Sean settled in a chair, leaning back indolently and stretching his long legs out in front of him.

'I'm surprised you haven't asked about the weather. I had a bet with myself that that would be your first question—when you could get out of here.'

'And can I?' It was impossible to disguise the lift of hope in her voice, the way her head had come up.

Sean's laughter was dark, a travesty of genuine humour.

'Sorry, sweetheart, you don't get away from me as easily as that. There was one day it didn't snow while you've been ill, and then it froze so hard that what few roads were opened will be positively lethal now. And I doubt if the snow-ploughs got to the lanes round here anyway. So I'm afraid we'd better resign ourselves to spending Christmas together at the very least.'

'Christmas!'

All the enjoyment Leah had been getting from the tasty soup vanished in a second. Her brain seemed to have come back into focus at last, bringing with it a new and very uncomfortable awareness of what Sean had been saying since he had come into her bedroom.

Three days he had said, and she had arrived here on...

'What date is it today?'

'December twenty-third,' was the lazily indifferent reply. 'Tomorrow's Christmas Eve.'

'But it can't be!'

Pushing her now empty bowl aside, she turned wide, shocked eyes on his composed face. Her mother would be frantic; she had expected her to arrive two days ago.

'I have to phone!'

Sean stiffened in his seat, the eyes that met hers coolly distant.

'No can do, I'm afraid.'

'Oh, don't give me that again! You may have fooled me the first time, but I know you have a phone.'

'Yes, but you can't use it.'

'And you can't stop me! Listen, you cold-hearted swine, I may be stuck with you, but I'm not your prisoner! You can't force me to— *Sean!*'

She broke off on a squawk of fear as, eyes blazing with cold fury, Sean sprang to his feet and covered the distance between his chair and the bed in three swift strides.

Thoroughly unnerved, Leah shrank back against the pillows. But Sean ignored her fearful response as he pulled the soup bowl from her nerveless grasp and slammed it down onto the bedside table with such force that she fully expected to see it shatter into tiny pieces.

Without a word, he swooped down on her, gathering her up into his arms with an ease that spoke volumes for the true strength of the muscles beneath the clinging sweatshirt.

'Sean!'

Her protest came weakly, too soft and shaken to have any real impact, and she didn't even know if he heard it. If he did, he ignored it ruthlessly, kicking open her door and heading across the landing towards the stairs.

'Sean!' she tried again.

'Shut up!'

Suddenly terrified for a very different reason, Leah subsided into silence, her hands instinctively clutching at the strong arms that supported her. One false move and they would surely fall, she told herself fearfully.

The thought of tumbling down the steep, narrow staircase sent a shiver of panic through her. They would hit the stone-flagged floor at the bottom—herself first, and then Sean's not inconsiderable weight.

But the next moment she was jolted out of her terrified reverie by the shocking realisation that Sean was laughing. She could feel his broad chest shake under her cheek, the rumble of his amusement sounding in her ear.

'Don't panic, sweetheart,' he murmured, in a very different tone from the one he had used earlier, his voice sounding warm and surprisingly soft. 'You're quite safe.'

As if to emphasise his point, his arms tightened round her, holding her close to the warm strength of his body.

And that was when everything changed. Leah found that she was shivering again, but this time with a very different sort of reaction, one that ripped through her already shattered composure, reaching right to its very core.

It wasn't fear that gripped her, making her pulse pound so heavily that it all but drowned the steady, regular thud of Sean's heart beneath her cheek. It wasn't even concern for her own safety, but something else entirely.

The sensations that seared through every nerve in response to the warmth of Sean's body reaching through the fine tee-shirt, the iron strength of the arms holding her, was one of pure physical excitement, nothing more. It set her blood ablaze in her veins until she felt as if she was back in the feverish delirium of her illness.

Her head was spinning in a way that had nothing to do with physical weakness. Unable to think, unable even to breathe properly, she was aware only of the effect that Sean's closeness was having on every one of her senses.

He wore no aftershave or cologne, and the clean scent of his skin so close to hers was more potently arousing than the most expensive of exotic perfumes. If she fitted her head back against his shoulder, looking up into his face, she could see the hard line of his jaw, that sensual mouth with its disturbingly full lower lip. From this side, that dreadful scar was hidden, his features once more the chiselled perfection that had won the hearts of so many ardent female fans.

Her mind hazing over, Leah felt as if she had once more lapsed back into the semi-consciousness of the past three days. Vague memories, previously forgotten, now floated to the surface of her mind like bubbles in a pond. She could recall Sean's face bending over her, hear his soft voice in her ear.

He had bathed her burning skin with something cool, held water to her parched lips. When she had been so weak and felt quite dreadful she had associated him with an overwhelming sense of relief and comfort, but as soon as she had improved at all he had reverted to being once more the coldly distant tormentor of her first evening in the cottage.

'Here...'

From the hall, Sean had turned left, into a part of the house she had never seen before. Looking around her, she couldn't hold back a faint exclamation of delight at the sight of the small, cosy room with its walls lined with bookshelves and a heavy, old-fashioned wooden desk set under the window.

But then her gaze focused on the telephone standing on one corner of that desk and her mood changed abruptly. The memory of the way he had lied to her was like the stab of a sharp knife.

'Right!'

Sean set her down on a large, high-backed, leather-covered chair and took a couple of steps backwards, away from her and towards the desk.

'Let's get this sorted out once and for all.'

Looking up at him, Leah could see both sides of his face once more, her eyes widening slightly as she took in the full impact of the scar.

Suddenly it was as if all the warmth had left her body, the heated delirium of only moments before fading and leaving her feeling lost and shaken. It seemed to her that the two sides of Sean's face could be taken to represent the two sides of his character, as he had shown it to her in their time together.

One side of his face was the face of an angel, a strong,

masculine beauty, with nothing soft or feminine about it. Years before, she had had an illustrated Bible in which the picture of the Archangel Michael had had just that same mixture of power and attraction that made up Sean's stunning features.

But the other profile was exactly the opposite. There the features were those of the devil incarnate, and in his personality, too, Sean was both of those things. One moment he was infinitely gentle and caring, the next darkly dangerous as any fiend. The trouble was that she didn't know which of the two she was facing now.

'If you won't trust me then perhaps you'll believe the evidence of your own ears.'

With a angry movement he dumped the telephone onto her lap and stood back, pushing his hands deep into the pockets of his jeans as he watched her with brooding expectancy.

'Well, go on!' he snapped when she hesitated, unsure of what he wanted from her. 'Phone someone, if you're so determined!'

Nerves jangled by this sudden about-face, Leah reached out a hand to the instrument. She couldn't believe he was actually letting her do this.

But as soon as she picked up the receiver she knew exactly what was behind his apparent change of mind.

The phone was dead. Instead of the reassuring burr of the dialling tone, all she could hear was the stark, unwelcome total silence of a disconnected line.

'The phone lines went before the electricity, three days ago.' It was a flat, emotionless delivery of fact, as unrevealing as his face. 'Luckily I managed to get through to the doctor before it happened. The last message in was the one the machine picked up just as you fainted. It was from Pete.'

His smile was a wry, ironic twist to his mouth.

'He'd realised, belatedly, that he'd given me an inaccurate description of Annie's car. In the state he was in, he'd forgotten that she'd acquired a new one at the weekend.

But since then the phone's been completely dead. Obviously they haven't got around to repairing them yet.'

It was too much. It had been hard enough at first, believing Sean's lies, thinking that the cottage had no phone and there was no way she could get in touch with her family. But to discover that there had been one here all the time, only to find that now, when she had finally got her hands on it, it didn't work, was almost more than she could bear. Her mother would be frantic, not knowing what had happened to her.

Weak tears welled up in her eyes at the thought, but, conscious of Sean's watchful blue gaze on her face, she lifted an impatient hand to dash them away.

'Hey, it can't be that bad.'

The unexpected softness of his voice, together with the apparently solicitous way he came to lean over her chair, were her undoing. They acted like a match set to dry brush-wood, burning away the moment of insecurity and setting free all the emotions she had stored up inside her.

'Can't it?' she flung at him, amethyst eyes flashing fire. '*Can't* it? Do you know what you've done with your nasty little scheme to kidnap me and keep me here? Can you even begin to imagine?'

His head had come up sharply, his eyes narrowing in swift response to her outburst, but not before she had caught a glimpse of something new in their bright depths.

She had caught him on the raw, she realised. She had actually got in under that armour-plated defence of his, found a chink in his otherwise perfect self-assurance, and made him *feel* something at last. The sense of triumph that brought added fuel to her already blazing anger.

'Do you know where I was going when you found me? I was on my way *home*! My mother was expecting me on Friday night, and when I didn't turn up she'll have rung my flat. Of course there'll have been no answer, so then she'll have rung Andy. And he won't know where I am either! So she'll be out of her mind with worry about where

I am. And if that wasn't bad enough she needs me so much right now, what with—'

'I rang her.' The quiet, firm words, inserted into a brief space in her tirade as she paused to draw breath, stopped her dead.

'You did what?'

'I rang your mother.' Sean destroyed her belief that she couldn't have heard him right. 'When I'd spoken to the doctor, and it was obvious that you wouldn't be going anywhere for some time, I checked your bag and found your parents' address in your diary. I told your mother you were safe here with me.'

'Safe' wasn't exactly the word, Leah told herself wryly, before the importance of what he had said hit home with an impact that stunned her.

'You did that!' Relief shone from her eyes, drying her tears, the desolate mood evaporating like a mist before the sun. 'Oh, that's wonderful! Thank you, Sean!'

Unthinking impulse drove her up out of her seat to fling her arms around him in a hug of gratitude.

'Thank you so much!'

The swift kiss she planted on his lean cheek was an equally instinctive gesture, simply out of relieved delight, and it obviously took him as much by surprise as it did her. For the space of a heartbeat he stood absolutely stock-still, blue eyes staring down into her face with a strangely blank, unfocused expression in them.

But then, just when she would have moved away, he woke from the momentary trance, reacting with a speed and strength for which she was totally unprepared. She was gathered up into his arms, imprisoned there without a hope of escape, and his hard mouth came down on hers, crushing it fiercely.

For a couple of seconds Leah's mind seemed to split in two. One half of it welcomed the furious passion of his kiss; the other fought against it with all her strength, desperately struggling against the wild sensation of burning hunger that threatened to overwhelm her.

The hunger won, making her sway towards him, parting her lips to the enticement of his tongue, feeling it tangle with her own. It was *her* arms that held them close now, *her* hands that tangled in the darkness of his hair, pulling his head down towards hers.

The movement brought her closer against him, to feel the heat and hardness of his need against her thighs. The blue tee-shirt had ridden up almost to the top of her legs, and left no barrier there to the heated exploration of his hands as they moved down over the curve of her hips and on to the smooth flesh below the soft cotton.

With a raw sound deep in her throat, she encouraged him to continue, the delicious sensations his touch was creating driving her to writhe in sinuous delight against the jut of his pelvic bone. After a moment's hesitation those caressing hands changed direction, moved upwards, sliding under the hem of the tee-shirt, closer...

But then with a jarring unexpectedness she found herself released as abruptly as he had caught her up. He let go of her so suddenly that for a second she was only supported by her own arms around his neck. And when he jerked back, breaking that hold too, she dropped down into her chair again, limp as a rag doll.

Beside her Sean swore, just once, but with a brutal savagery that made her flinch, her stomach lurching in fearful foreboding. But even as she tensed with apprehension he managed another lightning-swift change of mood, switching on the coolly indifferent façade he had used before. Stunned and dazed by the rollercoaster of emotions she had experienced in quick succession, Leah was hard pressed to know which of the darker sides of this man she hated the most.

'You don't need to thank me; it was the least I could do.'

Leah couldn't believe his unruffled calm, the cold precision of his words, when she was reduced to a shaken heap, her mind incapable of forming any rational thought. Was the man human? Or had she been deceiving herself to believe he had felt any of the blazing passion that had swamped her so completely?

But then she saw the faint tremor in the hand that swept his dark hair back from his face, the way his eyes were focused on a point somewhere above her head so as not to have to look into her face, and knew that his protective armour was not yet perfectly back in place.

'I would have phoned your fiancé too, but I couldn't decide which address was his. There seem to be at least four Andrews in there.'

So much for any supposed weakness, Leah told herself. If he had felt any such thing, it had taken only seconds to impose full control again.

That last comment had been laced with deliberate malice, and she had a sudden vivid mental image of the address pages in her diary and the number of entries on them under masculine names.

She could have disillusioned him. Pointed out that most of those names belonged to old college friends with whom she had done the Travel and Tourism course a couple of years before. On the last day everyone had swopped addresses with everyone else, and Leah had ended up with over twenty more entries in her address book.

Even though she had lost touch with the majority of her fellow students, apart from duty Christmas cards, sentiment had kept her from erasing the souvenir of what had been some of the happiest months of her life. But now Sean, in his nasty, biased judgement, had condemned her as an all-time flirt, with numbers of men listed in her equivalent of a little black book.

'So I'm afraid that dear Andy still doesn't know where you are—unless, of course, your mother lets him know.'

'I'm sure she will.'

It was impossible not to feel a rush of relief at the thought that Sean had not managed to contact Andy. If he had then he would have found out that the engagement she had laid claim to did not, as yet, exist.

Earlier, she had almost told him as much, but now a

newfound sense of self-preservation made her reconsider. She needed more time to sort out her own feelings before she dared risk having him know the truth.

And that opened the door to the real problem. The one that stilled her tongue and froze her thoughts in shock at the realisation that Sean had behaved as *she* should have done.

He had been the one who had considered the feelings of her supposed fiancé to the extent of being prepared to ring him up to let him know where she was, while Leah's first concern had been for her mother.

If she was strictly honest with herself she would have to admit that Andy had been the furthest thing from her mind, when, if she truly loved him, he should have been uppermost in it. And, that being so, how could she ever even *think* about accepting his proposal of marriage now or at any time in the future?

Leah shivered faintly as a sensation like the slide of something cold and wet moved slowly down her spine. In the past few months, when she had felt that everything she believed to be safe and secure in her life had been turned upside down, Andy had been her anchor, something to hold on to when things got rough.

Now it seemed that meeting Sean had taken even that, and with it her own conviction of the woman she was, and ripped it to shreds. Like the blizzard outside, he had swept over the landscape of her life and obliterated every familiar landmark, leaving behind a bleak and alien territory that she didn't recognise at all.

CHAPTER EIGHT

GOD, but he was all sorts of a fool!

Sean couldn't believe just how stupid he had been. What the hell had possessed him to react in such a way, responding to her like that?

He wasn't some hormone-driven adolescent who would snatch at any opportunity to grope a girl. If anything, given the sort of publicity his TV role attracted, he usually had the opposite problem. Women would do anything to get his attention, and more. Time and experience had taught him that the quick and emotionless sort of one-night stand they offered usually brought nothing but a strong sense of grubby dissatisfaction, which meant they just weren't worth the effort.

But with this woman all she had to do was to smile at him and he was putty in her hands. And when she had kissed him he had gone up in flames, unable to think of anything beyond the way she felt in his arms, the softness of her skin, the warmth of her lips on his cheek.

He knew she was like all the others. After all she'd told him that she was engaged—not that it seemed to matter to her. And yet, even knowing that, he still couldn't hold back.

He'd told her that, to him, an engagement was a binding agreement, second only to marriage vows, and he'd meant it. After the way Marnie had behaved, he had sworn that never, ever would he get involved in any sort of triangular situation with someone who was committed to another man. It had seemed so easy to stick to the promise he had made to himself—until now.

'I'd like to go back to bed now.'

Leah's voice intruded into his thoughts, drawing his attention to the way she sat huddled up in the big leather armchair. She looked disturbingly vulnerable and damnably feminine like that, he acknowledged unwillingly. The soft cotton of the tee-shirt clung to the curves and valleys of her body in a way that was guaranteed to raise his blood pressure alarmingly. That shirt had never looked as good on him, that was for sure!

But the softening effect of her physical appearance was counterbalanced by the coldness of her voice and a matching lack of warmth in her eyes, the stiff little lift of her chin as she addressed him.

'All right.' Reluctantly he forced himself to concentrate on practical matters. 'Do you think you can make it up the stairs on your own?'

She'd do it if it killed her. That much was written all over her face, firming the soft mouth and darkening her eyes.

And on this topic at least they were in total accord with each other. The last thing he wanted was to have to carry her again. He had only just been able to control his baser impulses after the first time.

But when she got to her feet it was obvious that her determination, strong as it was, was not enough. It was far outweighed by the physical effects of her recent illness, and what little colour she had leached from her face.

'I'm—not sure...'

It cost her a great deal to admit it, and she looked about as enthusiastic at the idea of the only possible solution to the problem as he felt. Despairingly, Sean closed his eyes against the images that assailed his thoughts.

Upstairs, he had come close to losing his grip on his temper. Well, if he was honest he *had* lost it, full stop.

Incensed by the accusation he had seen burning in her eyes, the obviously perverted objectives she had clearly attributed to him, he had blown his top. Furious that she should believe him capable of such perfidious motivation, he had acted on an impulse that he hadn't even considered in any sort of rational light, let alone thought through.

It had taken him precisely three seconds to realise his

mistake. By the time he was out of the bedroom, heading for the stairs, his whole body had been agonisingly aware of the soft, warm weight of her in his arms, the brush of her hair against his jaw. She had felt so good, so bloody good! Totally female and so sexy that it had been all he could do not to turn right round and carry her back to the bed.

That was why he had acted so stupidly just a moment ago. He didn't want that to happen again. To touch her was to risk fanning the flames that he had only just succeeded in reducing to still smouldering embers. It had taken the sort of ruthlessly brutal control that had left him aching in every nerve, each cell of his body bitterly resenting the way he had denied the fulfilment it sought.

With an inward sigh he forced his eyes open again, fixing his gaze on a point just past her head so that he didn't have to cope with her white-faced resolve.

'Look, I've got a better idea.'

His voice didn't sound as it should, and he swallowed hard to ease the sudden constriction in his throat.

'There's a fire in the living room; it'll be so much warmer than that ice-box of a bedroom. Why don't you lie on the sofa and I'll bring the duvet down to cover you?'

'I think I'd like that.'

'Then that's what we'll do.'

Did his own face mirror the relief that showed so clearly in hers? And did that mean that she had felt it too? That electric spark when they touched. The sudden heated awareness that turned the blood white-hot and sent it pounding through every vein, making the heart race as if after some violent exertion.

She let him take her arm, leaning against him for support as they made the short journey from his study and across the hall.

But that was all she allowed. At the first possible moment she jerked away from his hold, dropping down onto the settee with obvious relief.

'I'll get the quilt.'

He was glad of an excuse to get out of the room, fighting a determined battle for control as he made his way to the bedroom, taking the stairs two at a time.

Did she know what it had done to him when she had pulled away from him like that? He'd be willing to bet that she did, and that she had deliberately aimed for just such a reaction. But he hadn't liked the way it had made him feel. She had reacted as if he was something foul, something it would contaminate her to touch, and it twisted painfully deep in his guts to know she thought of him like that.

Yanking the quilt off the bed, he bundled it up in his arms and returned to the living room. Leah was still where he had left her, her slender legs curled up underneath her, her dark-eyed gaze fixed on the fire.

For a couple of seconds Sean paused in the doorway, just watching her, his gaze moving over the disordered tumble of her hair, the pallor of her cheeks, the long dark lashes that fringed those beautiful eyes. But then it fell lower, sliding over the swell of her breasts, down to the point where the creamy flesh of her thighs emerged from the soft blue of the tee-shirt, and he felt an unwanted heat build up in his lower body, driving him to make a sudden, uncontrolled movement that drew her gaze to him.

For a long, tautly stretched moment their eyes locked and held. Sean had the uncomfortable feeling that his thoughts must be written on his face, etched clearly there for her to see exactly what lustful images had been going through his mind. So it was a distinct surprise when she smiled suddenly.

'I was just remembering how, when I was a child, I used to imagine that I could see pictures in the flames if I stared long enough. It's been years since I had a real, open fire. There's only an electric one in my flat in London.'

'Pete thought I should have this one taken out and replaced by one of those gas-effect things.'

Sean dropped the quilt over her legs and lower body as he spoke. He thought about tucking it in around her, then hastily reconsidered, moving instead to sit in an armchair on the opposite side of the fire. He found he could breathe easier now that there wasn't quite so much of that luscious body on display.

'But I didn't agree. Exactly...' He laughed as her face showed precisely what she thought of the idea. 'They're not a patch on the real thing. But my brother is all for something to make the job quick and simple. He much prefers the easy life.'

'Except where his fiancée's concerned,' Leah put in drily, and Sean found his mouth twisting in wry response.

'Yeah, you could say that. His love-life always was amazingly complicated.'

'And now it's complicated your life too.'

A sudden memory of Marnie made him say quite honestly, 'Oh, I'm not so sure I can blame Pete for everything. I'm more than capable of screwing my own life up now and then.'

She wanted to know exactly when and how; it was written all over her face. But he had no intention of opening up on that subject, so he moved on to a very different topic.

'Your mother seems like a very warm, friendly sort of lady. I'd only spoken to her for a couple of minutes before she was treating me as if she'd known me for years.'

Leah's smile grew, softened, making his heart turn over with a thump.

'That's Mum, all right. She loves to meet new people and find out all about them.'

Suddenly a shadow came down over her changeable face, dulling those amethyst eyes.

'Was she OK?'

'Seemed fine to me.' He frowned, catching the uncertainty in her tone. 'Why—is there a problem? You said earlier that your mother needed you particularly now, so what's happened to cause that?'

Her frank surprise at the fact that he had even listened, let alone remembered what she had said, stabbed at him sharply. God, did she really think he was such a brute as to have been unmoved by her distress?

'She and Dad...'

'He's ill?' Sean queried when she didn't continue. 'Worse?'

Hellfire, just how would he square his conscience if her father had died? Had she been rushing home to be with her family and he had stepped in...? He couldn't live with the guilt if that were the case.

'Oh, no, nothing like that,' Leah hastened to reassure him, and the lifting of the pressure he had endured was like being released from what had felt like hours on the rack, for all it had only been a couple of seconds. 'But they've had problems. Then, six months ago, Dad just walked out. He said he needed space...'

'The classic line.' Sean laughed cynically. 'I believe my old man used that one when he took off, too. I've even been known to try it myself once or twice.'

That remark brought a reproachful glare from her darkened eyes.

'It happens, darling.'

'Not to my parents! At least I never thought it would. They were childhood sweethearts. They celebrated their silver wedding two years ago!'

'Then you were lucky.'

Suddenly restless, Sean got to his feet and took the poker to the fire. As he knocked the ash down to the bottom of the grate, the flames sprang up with renewed vigour.

'At least you grew up with two parents. Not everyone has that chance.'

'I know your father left, but that doesn't mean...'

'Nothing lasts for ever, sweetheart.'

Certainly not her own faithfulness, he reminded himself, thinking of how quickly she had forgotten her fiancé and turned to him. She might look so sweetly vulnerable now, on the exterior at least, but inside she was so very different.

Reaching for the coal bucket, he slammed several large chunks onto the fire.

'That's the way things are. Men and women just can't stay together for ever.'

'But surely it doesn't have to be like that?'

'Doesn't it? If you believe that then you're kidding yourself. If you want monogamy, marry a swan—or a seahorse. Aren't they supposed to mate for life?'

'*Mate!*' she repeated, obvious distaste curling her tongue. 'Most people would call it love!'

'Most people would! But personally I wouldn't believe them.'

He certainly wouldn't believe *her* if she claimed to love her fiancé. The thought of her hypocrisy seemed to curdle in his stomach, bringing a sour taste to his tongue.

There was nothing more he could do with the fire, but he knew he would find it impossible simply to sit opposite her and say nothing.

'Can I get you anything? Some tea, perhaps?'

'You don't have to dance attendance on me.' She was obviously still smarting from his use of the word 'mate'. 'I know you must feel I'm an awful nuisance.'

'Did I say that? You couldn't help getting ill. And besides, after the time I spent in hospital and then convalescing, I'm quite enjoying being on the opposite side, so to speak.'

'I'll bet you were a terrible patient.'

'The worst.' He couldn't help responding to the laughter in her eyes with a wry grin of his own. 'I've never been much good at sitting still and doing nothing. So I'm quite happy to play nursemaid for a while.'

The amazing thing was, he realised as he flicked on the kettle in the kitchen, that he genuinely meant what he had said. In the past couple of days, a great deal of the restlessness and dissatisfaction that had plagued him since the accident had eased. The dark moods had lifted, too, and with them the nightmares of the crash that had made it so difficult to sleep.

But then he just hadn't had time to brood, he reasoned. With Leah so sick there had always been something to do, and the effects of the appalling weather had only complicated matters.

At least that was the logical explanation, so why did he feel so uncomfortable with it?

'So, tell me some more about your family,' Leah said as she accepted her cup with a grateful smile. 'You've talked about Pete, but what about your mother? Did she take it hard when your father left?'

'"Devastated" would be the word,' Sean said, returning to his own seat on the other side of the fire. 'There she was, with one child already and another on the way, and suddenly she had to cope on her own. She just went to pieces. I did my best to take care of her—and Pete, when he arrived.'

'At nine? You must have been very mature.'

Sean's mouth twisted as he put his hands together, fingertips touching to form a steeple, his eyes fixed on their restless tapping. He had only mentioned his childhood very briefly, three days before, but it seemed she had registered everything he had said, and remembered every detail.

'I'm a Capricorn,' he said, aiming for a throwaway lightness. 'My birthday's January the twelfth. Someone once told me that Capricorns are born old.'

'I've heard that too. But they're supposed to grow younger in their approach to life as they get older physically. So if I came back here in—say—twenty years, you'd be more like my sixteen-year-old cousin, James. But then I suppose you'd think *I* was too old for you. Unless, of course, you're heavily into older women.'

The thought was disturbing. But even more unsettling was the fact that he, the Sean Gallagher who didn't believe in permanence, who thought that happy-ever-after was only for fairy tales, was actually considering what it might be like to be with the same woman—*this* woman—in twenty years' time.

'I'm sure any young man with red blood in his veins would still be interested in you twenty years from now.'

Startled violet eyes met his over the top of her teacup.

'But I'd be forty-five!'

'Oh, come on, you know perfectly well that you have

the sort of beauty that can only improve with age. Your eyes—that bone structure. Things like that will never fade.'

'Oh, please…'

Soft colour washed her cheeks and her eyes were brighter than ever.

'Such flattery…'

'I told you, I never resort to flattery,' Sean interrupted firmly. 'And certainly not with you. You must know the truth—see it every time you look in the mirror. Time will never rob you of your looks. It can only give you a different, deeper beauty.'

He meant every word of it, and from the look in her eyes she recognised his sincerity for what it was. But he also saw that he had somehow overstepped the unwritten rules by which they had been carefully rebuilding their relationship. In doing so, he had unbalanced the delicate rapport they had been creating between them.

For several long, intent heartbeats, violet eyes met blue, locked and held, communicating on a level too deep, too primitive for words. Then abruptly Leah blinked hard and dropped her gaze once more, hectic colour flaring high on her cheekbones.

'This tea is wonderful.'

'Coward,' he reproved softly, not knowing whether he was relieved or sorry that she was so obviously changing the subject.

That brought her eyes up again in a rush, her chin lifting defiantly as her burning gaze clashed with his.

'Not cowardice: common sense!' she said tartly. 'We both know this isn't real. It's just a sort of cabin fever, the result of being trapped together like this. But when it's over it will melt away again—like the snow.'

And she would go back to that fiancé of hers. She didn't have to spell it out; it was there in the flatness of her tone, in the way her eyes wouldn't quite meet his.

'Point taken,' he said stiffly. 'Would you like some more tea?'

'I'd love some.'

Her voice had a breathless quality, so that it came and went on the words like a faulty radio receiver.

'I was so thirsty.'

'Hardly surprising,' Sean returned with an equanimity that surprised even himself. It was light years removed from the way he was really feeling. 'After all, you didn't eat or drink properly for three days. It took endless patience even to get you to swallow a few sips of water.'

That brought her head up, her expression sobering swiftly.

'I really am grateful for the way you looked after me. You've been very kind.'

It was impossible to interpret what she was thinking, but the look in those velvety eyes, their sudden darkness, made the breath catch suddenly in his throat.

'You weren't a difficult patient. As I said, I was worse.'

It was supposed to lighten the mood. Instead it had exactly the opposite effect, bringing a frown of concern to her face.

'Was it so very bad for you?'

A lift of his shoulders tried to shrug off the past as unimportant.

'The hospital I don't remember too much about. At least, not at first.'

Her cup was empty again, and he got up to take it from her, painfully aware of the way her eyes watched every move.

When he had replaced it on the tray it seemed more natural, easier, somehow, to sit at the end of the settee, just by her feet, instead of going back to his chair. Leah made no objection to his change of seat, instead she adjusted her own position, turning to face him more directly.

'So it was convalescence that got to you? But by then your brother was with you.'

Sean nodded, his face grim as he recalled the dark days after he had woken to find himself in hospital.

'He stayed for weeks—waited on me hand and foot. In

the end I had to tell him to go. Here, let me sort these cushions out. You don't look at all comfortable.'

If he had hoped to distract her from this particular line of questioning, he didn't succeed. She waited quietly while he plumped up the cushions, leaning forward so that he could replace them behind her back, and then sank back again with a sigh of relief.

'That's better, thanks. So, was that when he told you about Annie?'

Sean nodded, lounging back against the arm of the settee.

'The young idiot hadn't said a word before then. But once he'd mentioned her he couldn't stop. It was Annie this and Annie that until I thought I'd go mad if I heard her name once more.'

Absently he rubbed at the scarred side of his face, frowning at the memory.

'I really thought—hoped—that it might work out for him.'

'You never know, it still could. It might just be a storm in a teacup, or a bad case of pre-wedding nerves. Does that hurt?'

Startled by the sudden question, Sean glanced at her swiftly, surprising a look of deep concern on her face.

'It aches sometimes,' he said slowly. 'Mind you, that's nothing compared to how it was when I woke up. It's ironic, really. At first I didn't realise what had happened, and then later, when I did remember, I just wished I could forget.'

Seeing the distress that flickered across those expressive features, he sat up hastily, reaching out to take her hand.

'Hey, it's all in the past. Believe me, I've mended.'

Were those tears in her eyes, making them glitter like polished jewels? Was it possible...?

'Sean, I'm sorry!'

'For what?' He frowned his confusion.

'The things I said earlier. I should never have accused you of hiding away here. I should have thought... I mean,

I don't know the full facts. I've no idea what really happened.'

'Do you want to know?' He startled himself as much as her with the question, not knowing he was going to say it until he heard it spoken out loud.

'I'm not prying.'

'It's OK.' Sean shrugged off her hesitancy. 'If you really want to hear, then I'll tell you.'

Suddenly he wanted her to know, but he couldn't have explained why. He couldn't have said, even to himself, whether he wanted to shock her with the truth, or if it was simply time he shared the whole experience with someone—anyone.

'It was a woman. A girlfriend, if you like, though there was nothing remotely *girlish* about Marnie. She was a woman through and through. We'd been seeing each other for around six months when I asked her to marry me.'

A stab of memory made him pause and grimace in distaste.

'I really believed we had something special—something exclusive. That illusion lasted another couple of months, until I found out that all the time she'd been with me there had been someone else. Another man. Someone she'd been seeing, dating—*sleeping with* even while she had my ring on her finger.'

He paused, shaking his dark head as if in disbelief at the memory.

'I was out of town quite a lot, filming, at the time, so I suppose she thought she'd never get caught. The poor sucker even believed she was thinking of marrying *him*! We had a hell of a fight about it and she flung my ring at me and stormed off—to go to him, I believed. But then I made the mistake of being seen with someone else. The next thing I knew, Marnie turned up on the doorstep.'

A sudden pressure on his fingers made him look down briefly. He had forgotten that he still held her hand, and her grip had tightened sharply as she listened.

'What happened?' It was barely a breath.

'The big reconciliation scene.' Sean's laughter was harsh. 'At first she was all sweetness and light. Told me how sorry she was—asked me to forgive her.'

'Did you...?' Leah put in, and his mouth twisted in cynical response.

'Oh, yes, I was fool enough to consider it. I tried. But deep down I knew it wouldn't work. I looked at her and I couldn't even remember what I'd seen in her; all I could see was the deceit, the lies. But when I tried to tell her it was over she went ballistic—screaming and crying, threatening to hurt herself or harm me. I made the mistake of choosing the time when I was driving her home.'

'No...' She had anticipated what he had been about to say.

'Yes.' He nodded grimly. 'On a country road, when there were no other cars in sight, she suddenly grabbed the wheel. She was hysterical—totally out of control. The last thing I remember was her yelling that if she couldn't have me, no one else would. That was just before we hit the tree.'

His smile was directed straight into her watchful pansy eyes, and was dark with the cynicism created by his memories.

'I spent the next two weeks in hospital and she walked away with a sprained wrist.'

'Oh, God!'

'Six weeks later, Marnie married someone else entirely. From what I hear, she's already been unfaithful to him too.'

Another assessing glance was slanted at her white, shocked face and then, realising he still held her hand, he slowly eased his fingers out of her grip.

'You asked,' he murmured sardonically.

But something had gone wrong. He had wanted to shock her and it was obvious that he had succeeded. But instead of the satisfaction he had anticipated he felt only a rather grubby sense of disquiet, wishing he had never opened his mouth.

He might not be hiding in the cottage, as she had accused

him of doing, but he now saw that, mentally at least, he had been doing something very close to that.

In the months since the accident he had kept the sordid events that had surrounded it totally to himself. But now he realised that that meant it had festered in his mind. To get it all into the open had been a private act of exorcism, and for some reason he had chosen Leah as the person to tell.

That thought lingered with him for the rest of the afternoon, making his mood uncomfortable and distinctly edgy. After a couple of attempts to revive the conversation, only to find herself rebuffed decidedly snappily, Leah gave up and retreated behind the defences of a novel she had selected from his shelves. That kept her occupied until late evening, when she stretched tiredly, hiding a wide yawn behind her hand.

'Time you were back in bed,' Sean said, getting to his feet. 'You don't want to overdo things on your first day up.'

'But I've been in bed for ages! I'm not sure I'll be able to sleep.'

'Then these should help.'

He reached for a bottle that stood on the dresser and shook out two of the tablets it contained.

'They're only very mild sleeping tablets!' he exclaimed when she eyed them with a look of dark suspicion on her face. 'I had some left from after my accident, and the doctor said you should take them at night in case your temperature went up again and you found it difficult to sleep.'

'There's nothing wrong with my temperature, and I don't like taking tablets! I hate the way they make me feel. I use them so rarely that they really dope me up.'

Sean sighed his exasperation.

'Well, if you're asleep you won't notice that, will you? They'll just help you get some proper rest. And you needn't think I'll be prepared to get out of bed and bring them to you in the middle of the night when you're feeling rough.

I want a good night's sleep, for a change, even if you don't.'

'Oh, all right! Seeing as you put it so very graciously!'

Snatching up the tablets, she tossed them into her mouth and gulped down the water he had provided.

'There! Happy now? I take back everything I said about you being a kind nurse. You're nothing but a big bully!'

'You drive me to it. So, can I offer to help you upstairs, or will that count as bullying too?'

He'd fully expected her to protest, to refuse outright. So he was genuinely surprised when she switched on a brilliant and almost convincing smile.

'That would be kind,' she said sweetly. 'Thank you.'

It was a relief to deposit her on the bed, an even greater one to pull the duvet over her and escape downstairs once more.

He had barely reached the kitchen when a thud on the floor above had him freezing in shock.

'What the...? Leah!'

Already his body had sprung into action, reacting even before he was aware of having mentally decided to move. He was at the top of the staircase again before he realised it, a chain of frantic thought running through his mind.

Had she fallen? Fainted? Why was she even out of bed? What if she had hit her head or worse? And what...?

In the doorway he came to an abrupt halt, his eyes going straight to the figure by the foot of the bed.

'*Leah!*'

At the sound of his voice she looked up, and relief at the fact that she was obviously unhurt clashed with the still uncontrolled fear that had set his heart racing just moments before.

'What the devil have you done now?' he demanded, his voice rough and harsh.

'I'm sorry. I knocked these over.' With a wave she indicated the small pile of books on the floor, two more in her hand.

'You— What possessed you to get out of bed in the first place?'

'I—wanted to go to the bathroom.'

'Then why didn't you just say?'

A glare from those violet eyes told him just what she thought of that.

'Surely I'm allowed *some* privacy? I thought I could make it on my own. I *could* have made it on my own if those books...'

'Give me patience!'

Released from the fear that had held him frozen, he marched into the room and came to her side. Picking up the books from the floor, he slammed them back down onto the table, his feelings spiralling close to anger, as if the sense of relief had been a spark that had set light to it.

'I take back everything I said about you being an easy patient! Do you ever do anything without arguing?'

'Pots and kettles!' Leah returned impishly. 'Of course I do. I'll have you know that at work I'm considered to be the most reasonable, easygoing...'

'You could have fooled me,' Sean put in sardonically.

'I— Oh, all right.' She gave a resigned sigh. 'So I'm not quite as strong as I thought. If I take your arm, will that do?'

'You only had to ask.'

With his arm around her waist he helped her out onto the landing and into the bathroom before he tactfully withdrew to his own bedroom.

Catching sight of his own reflection in the dressing table mirror, he saw the way the panic of moments before still lingered in the shadowed eyes, the lines etched round his nose and mouth, and moved to study his face more closely. He could barely recognise himself in the one that stared back at him.

What the hell was happening to him? How had he let this woman get under his skin in a way that no one else had ever done?

The sound of the shower running across the landing distracted him from his thoughts.

What now?

In a rush he yanked open the bathroom door to find Leah testing the warmth of the water with one hand.

'You're doing it again!'

'I want a shower.'

'You have got to be joking!'

'But I look such a mess! My hair—it's awful—lank and dull.'

She pulled at a strand of it and let it drop again with a grimace of distaste.

'You've been ill. You still are. You should be in bed.'

'But I feel so foul. I haven't washed properly for days, and I'm all dirty and sweaty and—ugh! I can't go to sleep like this. I'll feel even worse in the morning. I must have a shower.'

'Give me patience! You're not fit…'

'Oh, Sean, please!'

Her eyes were huge and dark, pleading with him to understand, and she came to put a hand on his shoulder, smoothing it slowly down his arm.

'It'll only take a minute.'

She was even closer now, both arms sliding round his waist, her head lifting so that the softness of her cheek rubbed against his.

'*Please!*'

Sean swallowed hard, knowing it would take a far more pitiless heart than he possessed to resist her entreaty. Already he could feel reaction twisting his guts into knots, depriving him of the ability to deny her. Did she know what she was doing to him? She had to…

But then he looked down into those wide violet eyes and realisation hit home like a kick in the stomach.

She hadn't been joking about the effect of the tablets. Even though they were only mild, they'd clearly combined with her residual weakness after the virus to highly potent effect. Leah was 'doped up', all right! She was almost out on her feet.

There was only one way this could be managed, but...

'Please!'

Hell and damnation!

'Right!'

Already one hand was reaching for the shower control, the other still supporting Leah. A sharp movement kicked off his shoes, then he tested the water to make sure it had reached the required temperature.

'OK, then—this'll have to go.'

He had peeled off the blue tee-shirt before she had time to realise just what he intended.

'Hey!' she protested, and now he could hear a faint slurring in her voice.

'Do you want this shower or not?' he demanded roughly. 'Then this is the only way.'

Lifting her bodily into the shower, he went with her, supporting her under the jets of warm water, closing his eyes for a moment against the unwanted feelings that assailed him as she clung to him, her hands tight on his arms.

'Sean!' she said again, but on a very different note this time. 'Your clothes!'

'They'll dry.'

He dismissed her protest almost savagely, knowing it was the only way he could get through this. He hadn't a hope in hell of stopping his body from reacting to her nakedness, her closeness to him, but at least remaining fully clothed might go some way towards disguising the fact.

'Now I'm going to wash you...'

The running water had plastered his hair down over his forehead, almost into his eyes, and he tossed it back with a rough movement as he reached for the shower gel.

'So if you could just think of me as you would a doctor, or a nurse. After all, that's what I've been these past few days. It's nothing personal, purely objective. If you can just hold onto me I'll be as quick as I can. OK?'

Her dark head, with the rich, smooth hair flattened

against the delicate shape of her skull by the water, nodded slowly, and her hands moved to fasten around his waist.

'Yes, Sean,' she murmured submissively, so submissively that it struck a very false note, instantly arousing his suspicions.

'Leah?'

One hand went under her chin to lift her face to his, the dreamy, unfocused smile telling its own story.

'Anything you say, Sean.'

Oh, God help me! Sean closed his eyes again briefly as he struggled with the sensations flooding through him. Think of me as a doctor! Surely any doctor who had thoughts like the ones filling his mind right now would be struck off the register pretty quick.

How had he ever believed that he could ignore the feel of her soft, warm, very naked body so close to him? That he could control the feelings sparked off by the slide of his soap-covered hands over her slick, wet curves, the rounded breasts, narrow waist and gently flaring hips?

It was bad enough when she stood stiffly in front of him, but it didn't take long before the warmth of the water and the feel of his massaging fingers took effect. Her eyes closed, the tension seeping from her body, and she relaxed against him with a small sigh.

'Oh, Sean, that feels so good!'

She moved against his hands, increasing their pressure on her body, the sound she made warmly sensual, like the purr of a small, very contented cat.

'So good... So very good.'

'Leah!'

The warning was growled deep in his throat as he moved his fingers to less provocative parts of her body. But her reaction to that was not what he'd anticipated.

'No!' Leah protested, her soft mouth forming a sulky pout. 'Don't stop!'

And she reached for his hands once more, pulling them back onto the warm, wet flesh of her breasts.

'I like that.'

So did he. Far too much.

'Leah!' He tried again.

'What is it?' she asked with a touch of petulance. 'Don't you fancy me any more? I thought you liked me—that you wanted...'

'You know I do. But now is not the time.'

'Of course it is! We have all we need. There's you and me and...'

'And you, my lady, are high as a kite!'

He almost laughed out loud at the irony of the situation. He'd said he'd wait until she was willing and he had meant it. But now here she was, as willing and as wanton as any man could wish for, and he couldn't trust it.

Hadn't she warned him of the effect the tablets might have? She didn't know what she was saying, and more than likely wouldn't even dream of suggesting any such thing if she were clear-headed. Only the lowest form of brute would take advantage of her present hazy state.

'High,' Leah echoed, with a catch of laughter in her voice that was almost his undoing. 'Must be the effect you have on me.'

Suddenly she frowned, her blurred gaze focusing on his now sodden sweatshirt.

'You can't take a shower fully dressed!'

Sean froze as her slender fingers slid under the hem of the soaking garment, trailing a path of fire up his chest. But when they slipped down again, closing over the buckle on the leather belt at his waist, he reacted as if he'd been stung.

'That's enough!' The words had to be forced from a throat that was tight with rigid control as he slammed a door in his mind shut against the heightened eroticism of his thoughts.

Ruthlessly ignoring the white-hot pulse of his blood, the ache in his body, he reached up and turned off the shower with a swift, violent movement.

'I was enjoying that!'

Ignoring her cry of protest, he lifted her out onto the mat once more. A couple of seconds later, with the sensual temptation of her body hidden underneath a large, soft green towel, he felt some degree of control return at last.

His heart gradually slowed from its urgent pounding; his breathing eased and became more regular. He even dared look at what he was doing, though when he saw the shake in his hands he knew that he was not yet back on the straight and narrow.

Still with one arm around Leah's waist, he reached for another, smaller towel and gently wiped her face dry before twisting it around her hair like a turban. Her delicate lids were still closed, but now they opened slowly and his heart clenched painfully as he saw that the deep purple irises were still dark and dilated with sensual pleasure.

'Better get you into bed before you collapse on me,' he muttered gruffly.

'Are you coming too?'

It was teasing, wickedly provocative, the smile that accompanied it almost totally destructive to his self-control. It was only by telling himself sharply that she probably had no idea what she was saying that he managed not to react.

'Don't be silly. You need to sleep.'

'Sleep? I don't want to sleep.' Her lips were close to his cheek, her breath warm against his skin, her voice husky with a promise of warmth and delight. 'I can think of a much better way to spend the night.'

'Leah, stop it!'

Sean repulsed her kisses with a violent movement, giving her a rough shake, just enough to wake her a little. His heart constricted as he saw the sensual look fade rapidly from her face.

'I'm sorry,' she said more stiffly. 'That was silly of me.'

'Your nightdress is dry; you can put it on again now.' Sean was determined to keep his mind on practical matters as he hurried her through to her bedroom. 'Here…'

He pulled it from a drawer and tossed it towards her, careless of exactly where it fell.

'You can get into it by yourself.'

It was a statement, not a question. He'd had enough. He

knew that he couldn't trust himself any further, and the prospect of helping her out of the towel and into the white lacy nightdress was positively lethal to his self-control.

'I'll put some dry clothes on and be back in a minute.'

What he really needed now was another shower—a freezing cold one—and then a hefty slug of whisky. But he couldn't take the risk that Leah might come into the bathroom if he did. There were only so many times a man could say no.

So he concentrated fiercely on stripping off his clothes, discarding the soaked sweatshirt and jeans and pulling on a cream cashmere sweater and nut-brown cords. He wanted to give Leah plenty of time to get dressed, and so he lingered deliberately, waiting a good ten minutes before he ventured back into her room.

To his relief she had not only put on the nightdress by herself but she had also got into bed. The covers were pulled up close around her neck and her eyes were tightly shut, her breathing soft and regular.

'Leah?' Sean kept his voice low, so as not to disturb her if she was asleep, and he breathed a prayer of thankful relief when there was no response. The tablets had finally taken effect and she was fast asleep.

She looked like a little girl curled up this way, her silky hair, still damp from the shower, spread out on the pillow. The temptation to run his fingers through it was almost too strong to resist. It was impossible not to recall the night before, when the electricity had failed and he had shared that bed with her.

Then she had been chilled to the bone, too cold to be aware of anything, and she had curled up against him as sweetly and innocently as a young child seeking comfort from a beloved and trusted parent. His mouth dried sharply as he recalled how he had lain there, unable to sleep, feeling her warm body curved against his, her long, slender legs entangled with his own, listening to the sound of her heartbeat.

'Oh, hell! Stop it, you fool!' he cursed himself in a violent undertone. 'Get out of here, now!'

He was relieved to find that at last his stupid body was actually prepared to obey the furious dictates of his mind and move.

But all the same he couldn't stop himself from turning back, just for a moment, and bending down to place the lightest, most delicate of kisses on her soft, sleep-warmed cheek.

'Goodnight, love, sleep well,' he whispered, before turning and hurrying from the room as if all the hounds of hell were after him.

CHAPTER NINE

LEAH woke the next morning to a wonderful sense of peace and well-being. Yawning and stretching like a contented cat in the warmth of her bed, she found herself smiling in pure delight.

She felt great! The lingering sickness and exhaustion of the day before had vanished, leaving her feeling clear-headed and totally relaxed. Sitting up, she flung back the bedclothes and swung her legs out of the bed.

It was then that she recalled the night before. The memory hit home with a force that jolted her upright on a rush of disbelieving embarrassment.

What *had* she done?

Sean had been so kind, so considerate. He had seen just how foul she felt and had acted in order to make her feel more comfortable. He had deliberately kept his distance too, making it all purely objective, no unwanted moves.

And how had she repaid him?

By trying, clumsily, to seduce him. By suggesting that he come to bed with her. And of course he had refused. He'd done it kindly, as considerately as he'd done everything else, but he'd turned her down quite unequivocally just the same.

Oh, God, she felt such a fool! How was she ever going to face him this morning?

Well, nothing could be helped by putting it off. She set herself to washing and dressing, pulling on jeans and the prettiest sweater she had with her, delicately patterned in blue and white flowers. She needed every bolster to her self-esteem she could find, she told herself as she made her way warily downstairs.

Sean was in the kitchen, pouring himself a mug of cof-

. He looked as if he had spent a less restful night that she had, with shadows lingering under the blue eyes. He also looked frankly surprised to see her up and about, but that was all, no trace of the embarrassment she was feeling in his face.

'Morning,' he said casually. 'You look brighter.'

'I'm feeling much better, thanks.' Leah couldn't bring herself to meet his eyes.

'Sleep well?'

'Wonderfully!' That much was true at least. 'What's the weather like today?'

Sean turned a brief glance towards the window, through which the white glare of the drifts covering the ground could still be seen.

'Well, it didn't actually *snow* any more during the night, but it didn't get any warmer either—at least, not warm enough to melt anything, that is. I expect any roads that were impassable before will be much the same now.'

'I don't suppose the phone's been repaired?'

'You suppose right.' Sean reached for another mug and began to fill it with coffee for her. 'It's still as dead as the proverbial dodo. Breakfast?'

'Yes, please. I seem to have got my appetite back.'

'Well, you certainly have more colour in your cheeks.'

They were like a couple of careful strangers, verbally circling round each other, making polite conversation but actually saying nothing, Leah reflected. Well, she'd take her lead from Sean. If he didn't want to mention the previous night, then she certainly didn't.

'So what did you plan to do today?' she asked, when, with her first solid nourishment for some days inside her, she felt rather stronger.

'Do?' Sean raised a deliberately sardonic eyebrow. 'What is there to do when you're stuck inside a snowbound cottage with no way of escape? Do you have some suggestions for our entertainment?'

'But it's Christmas Eve!' Leah forced herself to ignore the undercurrents she sensed in his words, the double edge he seemed to have put on that 'entertainment'. 'You can't let it pass like just any other day. We have to do something.'

'So what do you suggest?'

'Well, if I was at home we'd be putting up decorations and the tree.'

'Well, I'm sorry, but I happen to be fresh out of tinsel and baubles, and I don't have a tree handy...'

'But we can improvise!' Leah refused to let him retreat into the cynically negative mood of the first night. 'There must be—Oh, I know!'

Getting to her feet, she hurried out into the living room, pulling back the curtains to reveal the snow-covered garden.

'I thought so! Look...'

She hadn't realised that Sean had followed her quite so closely, and was startled to find him close behind her when she turned.

'Oh!'

It escaped on a small, choking gasp. Her heart seemed to be performing somersaults under her ribcage and her breath tangled in her throat. As she had been on that very first day, she was sharply aware of the height and strength of his body, the wide chest under the soft cream sweater, the length and power of his legs in worn denim jeans.

A slight, faintly bemused smile curled the corners of his expressive mouth, and she had to swallow down a disturbing urge to reach up and press a kiss on those beautifully shaped lips. That sort of thing was dangerous, she told herself furiously. Look where it had got her just days before!

'Look at what?' Luckily Sean was unaware of the wayward path of her thoughts. 'All I can see is snow, and even more snow. It's all very well on Christmas cards, but in reality it's downright dangerous and inconvenient.'

'You're not looking properly!'

Leah forced herself to ignore the obvious implication that, were it not for the snow, he would be only too glad to be rid of her 'inconvenient' presence.

'There are two wonderful holly trees out there. They've even got berries on them, so they'll be perfect. If we just collect some branches...'

She was heading towards the door as she spoke, but came to an abrupt halt as Sean caught hold of her from behind, strong fingers closing over her arm.

'No way!' he declared uncompromisingly. 'What sort of idiot are you? You've only just got out of your sick-bed, and you'd be risking pneumonia going out in these temperatures. I've had enough of playing nursemaid, even if you're not tired of being the patient.'

'Oh, I am!'

Her vehemence was a reaction against the sting of that last remark. He couldn't have made it plainer that his gentleness and consideration had only been for the duration of her illness. No more.

'And if I could get away from here, then believe me, I would. But, as I'm stuck, I'm simply trying to make the best of a bad job.'

'And that involves festive decorations?'

His tone implied that his mood, and therefore the atmosphere in the cottage, would be very far from the traditional one of celebration at this time of year.

'Oh, well, if it'll give you something to keep you occupied. Just tell me what you want...'

He wanted her quiet and out of his hair, Leah told herself, struggling to ignore a sharp stab of pain at the realisation. Well, that suited her. She'd concentrate on making the decorations and show him that she had no intention of making demands on his time or anything else.

In the end it was surprisingly easy. From the moment that Sean brought in armfuls of the holly branches she found herself absorbed.

Twisting the strands of greenery together to make a long garland, she draped it across the wooden mantelpiece, allowing several inches to dangle down at each side. Red satin ribbon that she had in her case in order to decorate her presents at home was turned into large bows at regular intervals along its length. And when Sean unexpectedly provided a box of creamy white candles she used them to add to the effect.

Next she moved on to the large Welsh dresser at the far side of the dining room, twining the variegated leaves around the bowls and plates that stood on it. As a centre-piece she arranged a huge display of the best of the berries in a large pottery vase. The work took her almost all day, but in the end she sat back and surveyed the result with some satisfaction.

'You're good at this.' Sean had just come into the room in time to see her smile of triumph. 'You must have some artistic talent I hadn't guessed at.'

'I always used to decorate my parents' house when I lived there.' A shadow crossed her face, draining the brightness from her eyes. 'There won't be anyone to do it this time.'

'Hey...' Sean had caught her change of mood and his hand came up to touch her cheek very softly. 'Your mother knows you're safe.'

'I just wish I could phone her and talk to her myself.'

That gentle hand dropped back down to his side abruptly, leaving a cold spot on her face where it had been.

'You never know.' Sean was turning away. 'Perhaps by tonight the phone will be back in use and you can contact her—and your fiancé,' he added pointedly.

'And Andy,' Leah echoed.

The other man would never be her fiancé now, she knew. She had always known that her relationship with him could not be described as a great passion, but she had cared enough for him to be able to consider his proposal of marriage. But from the moment Sean Gallagher had first ex-ploded into her life there had been no place in her thoughts for Andy.

She had tried to tell herself that it was only temporary. The initial shock of her accident had been followed by an enforced confinement which had pushed them into a hot-house relationship that her illness had only aggravated.

But now she had to face the truth. She was obsessed with
Sean, and helpless as a result. He had only to look at her
to fire the blood in her veins, kiss her to free the desire that
was always bubbling just below the surface of her mind
like molten lava in a barely dormant volcano.

'You've done wonders with this room. It looks positively
festive. But there's just one problem...'

Sean was obviously determined to change the subject,
and, disturbed by her own feelings, she was only too glad
to follow his lead.

'And what problem's that?'

'I doubt if I can provide a proper Christmas dinner to
match up to it. There isn't a turkey in the freezer.'

He looked unexpectedly rueful, so boyishly shamefaced
that she found her spirits lifting in response.

'No turkey?' she teased in exaggerated shock. 'Well,
what about plum pudding?'

A shake of his dark head gave her an answer, a grin
surfacing briefly.

'Mince pies?'

'Definitely no mince pies.' Now his expression was one
of distaste. 'To tell you the truth, I hate the things.'

'Sacrilege!' Leah's eyes were gleaming now, her eyes
alight with laughter to contradict her stunned tone of voice.
'You can't have Christmas without mince pies!'

Suddenly she took pity on him.

'I don't like them either—or Christmas pud. In fact I've
never liked dried fruit at all, so I'd be perfectly happy with
anything else.'

'We'll have to raid the freezer.'

As Leah nodded an idea struck her that made her eyes
sparkle, brilliant with delight.

'We can have whatever we want! Make up our own fa-
vourite meal. No one else will ever know that we didn't
stick to tradition.'

She pushed one last piece of holly into place with a sigh
of satisfaction.

'There! That's— *Oh!*'

It was a cry of distress and shock as she felt a sharp pain
in her hand. Glancing down, she saw that one particularly
rough-edged holly leaf had ripped a jagged cut along her
finger and thumb.

'Are you all right? Let me see.'

Automatically she held out the damaged hand, watching
with widening eyes as Sean took it in a gentle grip. Her
heart jolted in her chest, her mind hazing over, as she saw
him lift it, carrying it to his lips, kissing away the tiny red
beads of blood.

'Sean...' She could only manage a shaken whisper.

When he looked up into her face she could see how his
pupils had dilated until his eyes were almost all black, the
dark intensity of his gaze holding her transfixed. She was
barely aware of the fact that he had released her, or of her
action in lifting her hand to her own mouth, tasting him on
her skin as in a kiss.

'I...' he began, but she couldn't let him speak. The time
had come. If she was ever going to explain then it had to
be now, and she couldn't let anything get in the way.

'Let me tell you about Andy.'

The use of the other man's name was a mistake. As soon
as she had spoken she saw him stiffen, the warmth dying
in his eyes.

'Leah—' he began on a note of rejection, but she shook
her head violently.

'No, let me explain. It's not what you think. Really, it's
not! I told you that my mother and father had split up; it
shook me really badly. I thought that the foundations on
which I'd built my world had been shattered. I felt lost—
rootless. It was just around that time that I met Andy.'

At least he was still listening. That was something. She
had been afraid that he would turn and walk away from
her, but it seemed he was prepared to give her a chance.

So now the words came tumbling out in a rush. She was
desperate to have them said, to have everything cleared up
at last.

'He's quite a lot older than me—nearly forty—and I

think that was what attracted me at first. I realise now that I was looking for someone to hold on to, a shoulder to cry on. I also needed someone who could provide the sort of security I'd lost. I thought Andy was that person. I *wanted* him to be it.'

'And so you said that you'd marry him.'

'No! I haven't actually agreed to do so. He asked me, but I haven't said I'll do anything except think about what my answer will be.'

Cobalt eyes narrowed assessingly as Sean absorbed the facts she had given him. She could almost hear his brain working, thinking back over the past few days, centring on the time she had arrived at the cottage.

'So you claimed to be engaged in order to stop me...'

'As a protective device, yes. I...'

What was happening? This wasn't how she had expected it would be!

And what *had* she expected? Had she really believed that when she admitted to Sean that she wasn't actually engaged to Andy he would simply smile his relief and open his arms wide for her to fall into them? If she'd even dreamed of it for a single second, then she couldn't have been more wrong.

'I was scared,' she tried again, but already he was turning away.

'We'd better see about a meal.' She couldn't believe the flat, emotionless delivery of the words. 'Oh, and Leah...'

It was tossed over his shoulder at her, the throwaway inflexion somehow emphasising rather than disguising the suppressed anger behind it.

'The next time don't feel you have to resort to such subterfuge and storytelling. A simple no would have sufficed.'

How could she tell him that she couldn't have managed that no? Leah wondered as he strode out of the room, leaving her with no alternative but to follow him. How could she risk revealing that where he was concerned that particular word had never even entered her head?

Because Andy had never been able to spark off the sort

of physical excitement that Sean could create in her simply by existing. When he touched her she went up in flames, the heated response seeming to melt her brain so that she couldn't think, let alone find the mental strength to say no, and mean it.

'Take a look in the freezer and see if there's anything you fancy eating.'

Sean's supremely casual tone made it quite plain, without words having to be spoken, that the topic of Andy and her supposed engagement was firmly closed. There was nothing more to be said about it.

'And while you're at it you can check out the larder.'

This was going to be one extremely uncomfortable meal, Leah thought miserably. But as Sean flung open a cupboard door she caught sight of something that jolted her out of her despondent mood, bringing a sudden smile to her face.

'Tacos!' She pounced on the box in delight. 'I *love* tacos and chilli—the spicier the better. Do you have…?'

'Do I have any chilli?' Sean finished for her, pulling out a drawer in the freezer. 'My brother would laugh his head off if he heard you ask that question. Not for nothing do I have a reputation for having a cast-iron mouth in my family. You're obviously a woman after my own heart. How hot can you take it?'

'How hot can you make it?' Leah flung back, refusing to let her reaction to that easy 'woman after my own heart' show on her face or in her voice. It was just a phrase. It didn't mean anything.

But deep inside she knew that it did. It meant that Sean was getting to her in a way that Andy had never done, a way that she couldn't risk even letting herself start to consider. Forcing it to the back of her mind, she set herself to organising preparations for the meal.

'We should dress for dinner, make it something of a celebratory meal,' Sean surprised her by saying later when, with the chilli bubbling away in a pan, the salad prepared, and a bottle of red wine 'breathing' on the table, everything was almost ready.

'What are we celebrating?' Leah asked warily.

They had worked together in comparative ease, sharing every chore, sipping a glass of wine that he had poured. But now, with nothing more to do, she was unsure of just what his mood might be.

'You said it yourself. It's Christmas Eve—and you've recovered from the virus. All right, I admit it...' He had caught the sceptical glance she had turned on him. 'It's just an excuse to suggest that you wear the red velvet dress again. I never did get a chance to enjoy the full effect of it the last time.'

Because of the darkness of the night, or because he'd been so determined to take it off her? Leah found herself wondering, but strangely she found that she didn't care. She didn't know why Sean was offering her this 'celebratory meal', didn't know how far it was meant as an olive branch, or something else entirely. She only knew that it was an opportunity that she was going to grasp with both hands.

'Only if you wear something equally posh,' she tossed back airily. 'I don't plan on sitting in solitary splendour while you stay casual in your jeans. Does your wardrobe boast anything suitable?'

'I don't have a tux hidden away upstairs, if that's what you mean.' To her delight, Sean matched the lightness of her tone. 'There isn't much call for one on the Yorkshire moors these days. But I promise I won't disgrace you.'

'Well, in that case I'll go and put on my glad rags and paint my face.'

Excitement lifted her heart so that she practically danced up the stairs, humming to herself as she pulled the red velvet dress from the wardrobe and checked it over.

Thank God for Lycra! she thought to herself. It had survived the drive north and the wet conditions without any ill effects.

When her mind threw back at her the reminder that Sean's attentions had been far more likely to damage the dress than anything else, she refused to let the thought register. Instead she concentrated on the prospect of the evening ahead, and the new mood of peace that seemed to have grown between her and Sean.

With her skin still warm from her shower, she sprayed herself lavishly with the perfume she had packed in anticipation of a couple of parties at the houses of old school-friends.

She had also let herself hope that something might happen to bring her father back home in time for her parents' traditional New Year celebrations, she recalled, her mood sobering slightly, but perhaps that was asking rather too much. Still, she hated to think of her mother alone. If only she could ring her!

But that was impossible, and she forced herself to concentrate on her make-up instead. A light application of foundation and a touch of blusher removed the last traces of the pallor left by her illness, and subtle bronze shadow used with dark brown mascara highlighted her eyes. The final detail was a richly coloured lipstick that outlined and emphasised the fullness of her mouth, making it look warmly sensual.

Sliding into the red dress, Leah suddenly found that her heart was racing frantically as she recalled the way Sean had looked at her the last time she had worn it. It was impossible to forget his kisses and caresses on that night and all they had led to.

Did she want to risk a repeat of that reaction? she asked herself, considering her appearance in the mirror with a thoughtful expression. She knew the answer had to be yes when she met her own eyes in the glass and found that their violet depths seemed to be burning with an excited golden glow.

That was exactly what she wanted. But still she made one alteration to the way she looked, leaving her dark hair loose and soft around her shoulders in order to differentiate herself from the woman Sean had first encountered—the woman he had believed was his brother's fiancée.

Well, she was as ready as she would ever be. Sean was already out of the shower—she had heard the water shut off a few minutes before—so she had better head back downstairs.

On a sudden impulse she turned and, rummaging in the bottom of her case, pulled out a small, brightly-wrapped parcel from amongst the collection she had brought with her for distribution at home. It wasn't much, just a jokey present she had planned to give one of her friends, but, as everyone said, it was the thought that counted.

In the dining room, she placed the parcel at the foot of the large upright arrangement of holly branches by the hearth. It was the nearest she could get to anything resembling a tree. Then, feeling as nervous as a schoolgirl on her first date, she turned a bright smile on Sean as he came into the room.

That smile faltered, almost slipped at the sight of him so tall and handsome in the dark, perfectly tailored suit, pristine white shirt and subtle silk tie. She had never seen him so formally dressed, and it rocked her sense of reality.

For the first time he seemed like that luminous star of the acting world, the Sean Gallagher she had seen photographs of in newspapers and magazines. He was the man who attended film premières and award ceremonies, no longer the man who had patiently and gently nursed her through illness, who... Her cheeks flared at the recollection of how he had helped her to shower, and the clumsy attempt at seduction with which she had repaid him.

'Will I do?' Sean had caught her transfixed gaze, and he used the light question to break the sudden silence.

Leah could only nod silently, her throat closing over any words she might try to speak.

'And you know how you make me feel, dressed like that.'

His voice was low and intent, his eyes dark pools in the firelight, his gaze almost a caress in itself as he came to take her hand.

'I'm almost tempted...'

He caught himself up sharply, a faint shake of his dark head dismissing the thoughts he had been about to reveal.

'Come and sit down.' Gently he drew her towards the fire. 'We'll do this properly and have drinks first. What would you like? Sherry? Or there's…'

'Sherry would be fine.' Leah had found her voice again, though it sounded rough and hesitant as if from lack of use. She almost felt as if she might be ill again, her body temperature fluctuating wildly from burning hot to icy cold and back again.

She realised now what Sean was doing. Couldn't we start again? she had said. Act as if we were complete strangers. And he was behaving as if they were just that. As if this was their first date, so to speak, and, like a nervous suitor, he wanted to make sure everything was perfect.

Nervous suitor! She almost laughed aloud at the thought. 'Nervous' just didn't fit as a word to describe Sean, and as for *suitor*!

But she followed his lead when he started a conversation. She answered when he asked her questions about herself, listened when he told her of music he enjoyed, discussed books they had both read. All the time she felt faintly dazed by the ease with which he drew her out, the alcohol helping to relax her too, until she was smiling, laughing, eventually putting in her own questions and comments with increasing confidence.

'Tell me about your mother,' she said, when they had moved to the table and he was occupied filling the crisp taco shells with a tasty mixture of chilli, shredded lettuce and cheese, topped with tomato salsa. 'Did she ever get over your father's desertion?'

'Not for a long time. I really think he broke her heart. But then five years ago she met another man—a much younger man, as a matter of fact—and they were married last August.'

'You don't mind?'

'What? That he's not much older than me? Not at all.' Sean shrugged off the question. 'If he makes her happy, I don't give a damn if he's nine or ninety-four, or if he's purple with yellow spots. It's time someone in the family made a success of an emotional relationship.'

His words reminded Leah of a question that had been nagging at her for some time.

'You said that you started to see another woman...' she began hesitantly, shocked to find how much it mattered.

'After Marnie?' Sean's relaxed mood altered dramatically, his frown dark in the candlelight. 'That didn't last long.'

'You broke it off?'

In her mind, his declaration that nothing lasted for ever sounded with hollow significance, all the more so when she considered just why she cared about this other woman in his life.

'Correction, *she* broke it off.' Sean reached for his glass, swirling the wine round in the bottom of it as he stared down into the ruby liquid. 'After the accident.'

'She cared about the scar?' Leah couldn't believe that anyone could possibly be so shallow.

'She cared more about what it meant.' Sean's laughter was darkly cynical, his mouth twisting at the memory. 'The possibility of no more starring roles, no more sex symbol. She didn't like what it meant for her future.'

'But that's awful!'

He shrugged again, even more dismissively. 'At least she was honest.'

'Then she can't possibly have loved you!'

Love. It reverberated inside her skull like a warning bell, combining with the feelings she had already experienced and making her realise just why they were significant.

Love. That was the emotion she'd been struggling with for days, the feeling that had grown steadily inside her since that cataclysmic meeting on the snow-covered road.

'Love?' Sean enunciated the word as if it was in some new and incomprehensible language. 'I wasn't looking for love. Marnie cured me of that.'

'Oh, but you must have been! Everyone...'

'Everyone wants to be loved? Is that what you were go-

ing to say?' Sean enquired, a sardonic edge to his voice
implying a strong disbelief in the assertion. 'I don't take
that as a given. Not everyone is looking for commitment.'

'But…'

Oh, why couldn't she stop? Why did she have to give
so much away?

'But you are,' he interjected when her nerve failed her.

His firm pronouncement had an effect like a blow to her
heart, bruising it painfully.

'Was that what your fiancé offered you? Love and de-
votion and happy ever after?'

Love. Hearing the word spoken in that beautiful deep
voice sparked off memories she wasn't emotionally
equipped to handle. From a hidden corner of her mind came
the recollection of how, on the previous night, she had
drifted to sleep while waiting for him to come back into
her room. At some point she had sensed his presence beside
her bed, but she had been too tired even to open her eyes
or lift her head.

Lying there, half-conscious, she had heard his soft words,
felt the even softer kiss. 'Goodnight, love…' he had said,
but anyone who had heard his cynical declaration that love
was just a myth, a fantasy, could not escape the truth. She
wasn't his love and never would be.

'I told you, Andy isn't my fiancé!'

She concentrated hard on spooning chilli into another
taco shell, almost as if her life depended on not spilling a
single drop.

'So you did.'

He was refilling their wine glasses with a generous hand
as he spoke, and, well aware that she had already had quite
enough, Leah tried to protest.

But as she had just taken an enthusiastic bite of her food
her mouth was full of the spicy mixture and the result was
just an incoherent murmur. It turned rapidly into a cry of
annoyance as the crisp corn shell splintered, squeezing the
meat sauce out over her hand.

Dropping the taco back onto her plate, she started to lick

her fingers clean, freezing suddenly as she became conscious of Sean's intent blue gaze.

'Did you know you had tomato stains on your chin?' The question was warm and soft, laughter lifting it at the end. 'Here, let me...'

With his napkin he carefully wiped away the mess from below her mouth.

'And there's some more here—you're in a real state!'

The white linen moved to her top lip, brushing softly over its full outline.

Leah's heart seemed to stand still suddenly, then jerk back into action at an accelerated rate. Swallowing hard, she drew in a deep, uneven breath.

'That's the trouble—or the fun, depending on the way you look at it—with this meal.' She struggled to inject a lightness she was far from feeling into the words. 'It's so amazingly messy that it's the sort of thing you can only eat with someone you're very close to, and so can be totally relaxed with, or someone you never want to see again, so you don't mind if you make a real fool of yourself.'

Too late she saw the trap she'd dug for herself but couldn't retreat from. She could only wait as Sean squeezed his napkin into a ball with one hand, his eyes fixed on her face, blue eyes very dark and serious.

'And which of those would you say describes what we have?'

'I...' She licked dry lips nervously. 'I don't know.'

'Which one would you like it to be?' It was noticeably softer, an octave deeper.

'I...'

She couldn't find the words to answer him, and she couldn't look anywhere but into those mesmerising eyes, seeing in their darkness the reflection of the flicker of the candlelight.

'Perhaps you'll find another question easier to answer. So, tell me, when you get out of here—because this snow can't last for ever—what are you going to do?'

Leah's hand had lifted to reach for her glass, but now it

froze again. She could try to dodge the issue, to pretend that she didn't know what he meant, but to do so would be craven and weak, and Sean would know it too.

He wasn't asking her about her career or her parents, or what she would do about her car, but about one very important and specific issue.

But it wasn't a simple issue to resolve. The answer to his question came trailing complicated strings of repercussions that would affect every part of her future, possibly even the whole of her life.

'Leah?' he prompted harshly when she hesitated, eyeing him like a terrified rabbit transfixed by the lights of an oncoming car. 'You must know. What answer are you going to give to Andy?'

Leah drew in a deep, shuddering breath. And suddenly it was so very simple. It was as if a light had gone on inside her head, one that illuminated everything around it with startling clarity.

She didn't have to think or to question. There was no room for any doubt at all in her mind. There was only one possible answer.

After all, hadn't she known this deep down from the very start? Hadn't she known from the moment she had realised that simply being with Sean could drive all thought of Andy from her head that what she felt for the other man was not love but a sense of gratitude and comfort, seeing him as a support at a difficult time?

'No,' she said with absolute conviction. 'I'm going to tell him that no, I can't marry him.'

She knew from Sean's expression, from the sudden blaze of reaction deep in his eyes, that he understood all that was involved in her answer, everything that was behind it, unspoken and yet so very clear.

'Leah...'

And then as Sean pushed back his chair, his midnight-blue gaze still fixed on her face, she saw that there was one more thing she had to do to make sure there was no room left for doubt.

'And the answer to your other question is yes,' she said firmly and confidently, no trace of hesitation in her voice. 'Saying no to Andy means I'm saying yes to you.'

The chair-legs scraped on the floor as he stood up in a rush, his hands going out to pull her up beside him.

She moved with him, no room for hesitation or even for thought in her mind. She was all need, all hunger, her body instantly on fire at the touch of his hands, the fierce pressure of his lips on her mouth. And that fire was fuelled by the absolute certainty that this was right. This was what she had known must come, what was as inevitable as the beat of her heart.

There was no time for gentleness, for care, for finesse. Each was as hungry as the other, greedy for the touch of skin on skin, for the heat of each intimate caress felt without the barrier of clothes.

Leah's hands were as urgent on the buttons of his shirt as his on the velvet of her dress. As she tugged them free from their fastenings with a trembling impatience he pushed up the clinging fabric of her skirt, hot fingers curving into the soft flesh at the tops of her legs, pressing her hard against him.

'Don't you think we'd be more comfortable upstairs?' Sean's question was a hoarse, shaken laugh against her mouth, the words as raw and uneven as every shuddering breath he took.

'Do you *care* about comfort?' Leah muttered back. 'It's too late for that—far, far too late.'

His sigh was an acknowledgement of the truth of her compelling assertion. Neither of them could wait, nor delay what was happening a moment longer.

There was no need of foreplay, or any caress used to heighten the anticipation, awaken the senses to the prospect of the pleasure to come. Every moment since their first meeting had been building up to this, Leah thought raggedly. Each minute they had spent in each other's company had added further fuel to the already blazing fire of need until it had turned into this most violently frenzied inferno that nothing could subdue, nothing could control.

And so she moved with Sean when he half walked, half carried her towards the hearth and laid her down on the rug before the fire. With yearning hands she helped him ease the velvet dress from her body, writhing sensuously as she felt the warmth of the flames on her skin, the pale flesh dappled with firelight and shadow.

'You too,' she murmured with a mock petulant frown as he came down beside her, still partially clothed, the shirt she had unbuttoned hanging loose over his wide chest.

'Me too,' he whispered in laughing agreement.

The shirt was swiftly discarded, shrugged off even as his impatient mouth sought the warm curves of her breasts. Somehow he managed to continue to kiss her while his hands dealt with the fastenings on the rest of his clothing, tossing it aside with careless impatience as he moved to crush her closer to him.

'Better?'

'Much better!' It was a sound of dark contentment deep in her throat. 'And now...'

'No!'

Strong hands closed over hers when she would have reached for the fastening of her silky bra, his fingers manacling her wrists and imprisoning them on the rug above her head.

'That pleasure is *mine*,' he growled, arousal thickening and roughening his voice so that it sounded more raw, more huskily male than ever before. 'Lie still and let me handle things.'

She tried. She tried her damnedest to control the buzzing impatience that jangled every nerve-end, set her pulse searing through her veins. But when Sean's free hand didn't give her the sensation she sought, instead smoothing slowly and deliberately down the side of her ribcage, along the curving indentation of her waist and along the delicate band of lace that topped her briefs, she couldn't stand it any longer.

Her body bucked beneath that tormenting touch. Her eyes blazed with a need she didn't even try to hide from him. And a wild, keening sound escaped her lips before she flung a muttered protest into his shadowed face.

'Patience, darling, patience!'

The trace of laughter in his voice was the last straw.

'I'll give you patience!' she declared, desperation giving her the strength she needed to wrench her hands free from his restraining grip. 'Let's see how *patient* you can be...'

With a smile of triumph she felt him shiver under the slide of her fingertips, heard the groan of surrender that formed in his throat as her hands crept lower...lower... When at last they closed around the most intimate part of his body he expelled his breath in a violent curse that delighted her with its obvious evidence of his loss of control.

'You little witch!'

Even as he shuddered in response to her touch, his hands were busy. Wrenching away the last flimsy barriers between them, he discarded them into the darkness beyond the firelight before setting himself to wreak a sensual revenge on her.

First his hands and then his lips played over her body in a deliberately tormenting progress that had her crying out her need in a sharp, shaken voice.

Only then did he ease his body over hers, urging her thighs apart with the pressure of his. Supporting his upper body on his arms, he watched her face as he eased himself into her, the glaze of a fiercely reined-in passion darkening his eyes as he saw her twist beneath him in response.

'Is this what you wanted, Leah? Is this...?'

'Oh, yes!' She was reaching for him even as she spoke, her hands closing over his shoulders, drawing him down to her so that she felt the full weight and strength of his body over hers. 'Yes, it's what I've always wanted...always...'

But when he moved again all power of speech left her. She could only feel, exult in the pulsing strength of him inside her and in her own soaring response. Slowly, inexorably, the rhythm built and built, taking them both higher and higher until there was nowhere else to go but over the edge and into the very heart of the conflagration, letting it burn them up completely.

Afterwards, she curled up in his arms, unable to speak, unable even to think. And Sean just held her, as if he too had been shaken by the intensity of what they had experienced, as if he too needed time to come to terms with it.

From there she drifted into sleep, stirring only reluctantly when she felt a hand on her shoulder and heard Sean's voice in her ear.

'Leah,' he whispered huskily. 'Leah, wake up.'

'Mmm?' She didn't want to move. She wanted to stay where she was, drifting on the warm, gentle sea-swell of contentment that seemed to flood her whole body.

'Leah,' he persisted, more sharply now. 'There's something I want to show you.'

Yawning, blinking sleepily, she sat up and looked round her expectantly. Beside her, Sean had already pulled on his trousers and shirt, leaving the latter unbuttoned over the width of his chest.

'What?'

'Not here,' he laughed. 'Outside. Here, you'll need this.'

Reaching for the cream sweater he had left lying over the back of a chair earlier that evening, he pulled it over her head and helped her slide her arms into the sleeves.

It was far too big for her, the creamy cashmere falling to her thighs like a soft knitted tunic. Looking at her, Sean's eyes darkened again, and a groan that was a blend of delight and torment sounded in his throat.

'God, but you would tempt a saint! Come here!'

She thought he wanted to kiss her, but instead he pulled her to her feet and swung her up into his arms, making her gasp with shock.

'Sean!'

'Hush, sweetheart. There's something very special I want you to see.'

He carried her through to the kitchen, gently setting her

back onto her feet before opening the door and gesturing with one hand.

'Look…'

'Snow!' Leah's disappointment sounded in her voice. 'You brought me out here to—'

'No.' Gentle fingers came under her chin, lifting her face until she was staring at the sky. *'Look!'*

And then she saw it. The pale, gleaming shape of the full moon high in the clear sky, and at one side the dark shadow, like a bite taken out of it, slowly, gradually encroaching on the light.

'An eclipse!' Leah let her breath escape on an entranced sigh. 'I've always wanted to see one, but never had the chance!'

How long they stayed there, arms around each other, their eyes fixed on the heavens, she had no idea. She was only aware of the magical phenomenon before them, watching transfixed as the darkness slowly crept over the silver circle of the moon until its light was almost blotted out, only the faintest glimmer showing at the outermost rim. Then, at last, she turned to the silent man beside her.

'Oh, Sean! That was magical!'

'Not quite the Christmas star.' He smiled. 'But close enough.'

But as he bent to brush a swift, delicate kiss across her parted lips his dark head blotted out the sky, and suddenly an icy, uneasy sensation crept over Leah's skin like frozen footprints, making her shiver in uncontrollable response.

'You're cold!' Immediately Sean was all concern. 'I've kept you out too long!'

'I'm OK,' Leah managed, but that feeling of uncertainty still lingered, like a premonition of disaster, draining her voice of all conviction and making Sean frown swiftly.

'I'm a fool! I forgot that you've been ill, Leah, I'm sorry. It's time I took you to bed.'

But not to sleep, his eyes promised, and as the warmth

of his smile enclosed her, his arms folding round her, Leah pushed away the dark shadow of foreboding and let herself be lifted up once more and carried into the house and up the stairs.

CHAPTER TEN

SEAN woke with a contented smile on his face. A smile
that grew into a wide grin as the movement he made
brought him into tingling contact with the soft, warm female body curled up alongside him.

Leah. Just the sound of her name was like a song inside
his head. A song that echoed through his heart and along
every vein, tantalising other, more sensitive parts of his
anatomy.

'Leah,' he murmured softly, reaching for her.

But he left the movement uncompleted as a new and very
different sound impinged on his consciousness. A noise he
hadn't heard for so long that it took him a while to register
it properly and recognise exactly what had made it.

Rain. Large, heavy drops pattering steadily onto the roof,
their regular pounding almost shocking after the silence of
the past snow-bound days.

Rain. The implications of that fact hit home with a jarring shock, jolting his head up off the pillow, sending his
gaze swiftly to the window.

Was it his imagination, or had the white glare of the
snow that had showed through the slit in the curtain eased
already?

Moving slowly and carefully, so as not to disturb the
sleeping girl, he slid out of the bed. His bare feet making
no sound, he crept from the room, collecting his clothes as
he went.

He wasn't prepared for the sight that met his eyes when
he opened the front door. The pristine drifts of snow no
longer existed. In their place was a muddy, churned-up
swamp, patched here and there with grey-white lumps of

stubbornly resistant ice. Clearly the rain had been falling for far longer than he had realised.

But then, of course, neither he nor Leah had been aware of very much for the past... He checked his watch. For the past sixty or so hours. Christmas Day and Boxing Day had come and gone unnoticed by them, as had the first twelve hours of the twenty-seventh.

If the truth were told, they had barely even been aware of whether it was day or night, so lost had they been in their own secret, sensual little world, in which nothing mattered beyond each other and the fires of passion they lit between them. They had only emerged from his bedroom long enough to eat. But the sandwiches and coffee they had snatched had tasted far better than any turkey dinner with all the trimmings could have done.

The grin that had been on his face when he had woken surfaced again at the thought of Leah lying asleep upstairs. He'd make her some tea—possibly even breakfast on a tray—and take it up to her. He would kiss her awake slowly, gently, and with any luck they'd forget all about food all over again.

A loud, shrill sound echoing through the stillness of the morning startled him out of his reverie. For a couple of seconds he stood confused, not recognising it. But then sudden realisation had him heading for the study.

When had the telephone lines been repaired? Obviously that, too, was something that had happened while he and Leah had been otherwise occupied.

'Sean! Hi!'

He scarcely recognised his brother's voice, it was so completely different from the dull, lifeless tones he had last heard Pete use.

'Happy Christmas, big brother! Rather late, but what the hell?'

'Pete?'

It was a struggle to drag his thoughts back from the heated daydream of Leah and the anticipation of a sensuous exploration of her body on which they had been lingering.

'Where are you ringing from?'

Was his brother even now on his way to the cottage? And if he was...

'Home,' Pete's cheery voice informed him. 'Where I've just spent the most wonderful Christmas of my life. I've never had so much fun. And Annie—'

Annie? The name reverberated in Sean's skull like the after-effects of a heavy blow.

'Hang on a sec, kid! Did you say *Annie*?'

'Sure did! She's right here with me, has been for the past six days. Oh, I know I should have told you, and put you out of your misery, and I tried to but I could never get through.'

'The lines came down in the blizzard.'

Sean's response came vaguely. He was thinking back frantically, reckoning up dates. Six days. The day Leah had become ill, when the phones had been cut off.

'It was all a damn stupid mistake.'

Pete was blithely oblivious to his brother's stunned silence, his evident happiness making him insensitive to everything else.

'The silly girl got into a terrible panic. She'd convinced herself that she wasn't good enough for me! *Her* not good enough! Can you believe it? And so she made up the whole stupid story of another man, thinking that she was setting me free, when, as you know only too well, the last thing on God's earth I wanted was my *freedom* without her!'

As Sean managed some sort of inarticulate murmur that might just have been agreement, he heard light footsteps coming down the stairs. Leah was awake and out of bed.

'She'd planned on going home to her parents to lick her wounds, but the snow was so bad that she had to turn back. And when I went round to her flat she was...'

The rest of the story faded into a blur as the study door opened and Leah appeared, her face still flushed from sleep, her dark hair loosely dishevelled around her shoulders. A navy towelling robe—*his* towelling robe, Sean noted with a jerk of his heart—was all that covered her nakedness.

Her smile made his mouth dry and he held out his hand to her, his heart kicking again as she came forward so eagerly to take it, her fingers linking softly with his.

With a movement of his arm, he twisted her round so that she was pressed close up against him. Her back was against his chest, the rounded softness of her behind cradled by his hips where she must surely feel the growing hardness that betrayed his body's immediate response to her. Her hair brushed his cheek as he touched his lips to her temple.

Who? Her mouth formed the question silently as she nodded towards the phone in his hand.

'Pete.' It was just a murmur, his hand sliding over the receiver to cover the mouthpiece. 'And guess what? Annie's gone back to him already, so it was all for nothing.'

'Sean?'

His brother had finally become aware of his lack of response, and with a grimace of resignation Sean realised that his abstraction had alerted the younger man's suspicions.

'Why don't you go and make some coffee?' he whispered to Leah.

Reluctantly he released her, giving her a gentle push towards the door.

'I'll join you as soon as I finish here.'

He watched her walk away, fascinated by the grace of her movement, his gaze lingering on the rounded curves of her body, the sway of her hips. The thought of her wearing the same robe that only the day before had been covering his own body was somehow so exciting, so intimate, that he couldn't focus his thoughts on anything else, even after the door had closed behind her.

'Sean!' Pete was obviously intrigued now. 'What's going on there? Who were you talking to?'

Silently Sean cursed himself for not pressing the secrecy button. His attempt to cover the receiver had obviously not been enough.

'No one important,' he hedged, knowing he was not yet ready to share this special something he had with Leah with anyone else.

It would come soon enough. Now that the weather had changed and the snow was clearing, their isolated hideaway would not stay that way for long. Already the restoration of the phone had brought the outside world back into their private sanctuary.

'Let's just say she's a little Christmas present I've given myself.'

'I see.' Pete's response was an appreciative chuckle. 'You kept that hidden, brother mine. But then you always were much better at secrets than me; you never used to hunt out your presents before the big day.'

'Well, don't put too much importance on that.'

Sean aimed for a casual indifference, not knowing whether he was convincing his brother or not.

'As I remember it, on Christmas morning it was always the *unwrapping* that was the exciting part of getting presents. Once you knew what the present actually was, it often lost its appeal. Because, quite frankly, sometimes the wrapping on a parcel is very deceptive, its colour and brightness hiding something you really don't actually want to keep.'

'But as *I* recall,' Pete put in, 'You always kept your very best presents to yourself, while I just couldn't wait to let everyone know what I'd got.'

'It seems we're not so very different now we've grown up,' Sean admitted, knowing his brother would understand the significance of the admission.

'Well, I'll leave you to your *present*.' Deliberately Pete emphasised the last word. 'I just wanted to let you know that the wedding's back on again, so I'll see you in the New Year. Why don't you bring that special someone along with you?'

'I don't want to commit myself to anything like that,' Sean put in hastily. After all, what were six days on which to build anything more permanent? They had been six magical days, it was true—or, at least, three of them had— but he had yet to see what would happen when the real world invaded their idyllic existence once more.

'She's not the type I'd like to expose to a family gathering.'

'Typical Sean,' Pete laughed. 'If you ask me, it sounds like this girl's knocked you for six. In fact, you've fallen so hard that you don't even know what's hit you yet.'

Oh, but he did, Sean reflected as he put the phone down again a few moments later. He knew just what an effect Leah had had on him. The problem was what he was going to do about it. After all, when you've been determined to deny that true love exists, how do you recognise if what you're feeling actually is the 'real thing'?

All he did know was that he'd been apart from Leah for quite long enough. He wanted to be with her again, see her smile, hear her voice, kiss her...

He was on his way to the door when a sudden thought struck him and he turned back hastily, reaching for the phone again.

'Your coffee's almost cold.' Leah's tone was unexpectedly stiff and distant, making Sean frown in surprise. He hadn't kept her waiting all that long.

'I couldn't get away, and then I had to make another phone call—for your benefit this time.'

'My benefit?' She was moving to empty the cooling coffee down the sink, refilling the mug and carrying it through into the sitting room. 'What do you mean?'

'Your car.'

Sean took the mug she held out to him with a swift smile of gratitude.

'I rang the garage and asked them to collect it as soon as possible, check it over and sort out any problems the accident had caused. They'll ring back to let you know when it's ready.'

'That was kind of you. Thanks.' Her reply was distracted, the smile that accompanied it a brief flashing on and off, like a neon sign.

'And now that the phone's working you can ring your

mother, let her know you're OK. You can call work as well, if you need to. When are you due back at the agency?'

'Not till after the New Year. I took some extra holiday especially to be with Mum.'

Sean frowned at her response, not in reaction to anything she had said, but because of the way she'd spoken. She'd sounded like a robot, churning out carefully programmed replies without emotion or intonation to give them any sense. Putting down his cup, he beckoned to her with his hand.

'Come here.'

But when she didn't move, watching him instead with eyes shadowed by something that looked worryingly like suspicion, he frowned again, more darkly this time.

'Is something wrong?'

'Wrong?' she echoed with a touch of satire. 'You could say that.'

Her head had come up, her voice sharpening. But there was a betraying unevenness in the middle that revealed an inner conflict she was trying to hide.

'Where would you like me to start? How about with the fact that your brother's fiancée is back with him so "it was all for *nothing*"?' She emphasised the last word bitterly.

'Leah…'

'So, just *what* was "all for nothing"? Your kidnapping of me and keeping me here? Or perhaps your seducing me—the last couple of days—that "little Christmas present" that you've given yourself?'

So that was what was troubling her.

'You weren't supposed to hear that.'

And, having heard her quote his words back at him, he sincerely wished she hadn't. They sounded much worse than he could have believed, far more insulting than he had ever meant them to be.

'Oh, I'll just bet I wasn't!' Gold sparks flashed in the amethyst eyes, her chin coming up defiantly. 'After all, I don't matter. I'm just "no one important"!'

The acid with which she laced those dreadful words

caught him on the raw, because he didn't know how to defend himself without getting into deeper water that he wasn't ready to swim in yet—if, in fact, he ever would be.

Turning away from her, he walked to the window and stared out at the rain, heavier now than ever before.

'So you were listening at the door!' With no time to think, he hid his confusion behind a show of anger. 'Well, you know what they say about eavesdroppers never hearing any good of themselves!'

'I was not eavesdropping!'

'Oh, weren't you?'

Swinging round to face her, he met the accusation of her violet eyes head on.

'Then what else were you doing there? I seem to recall that I asked you to make coffee.'

'And I don't *recall* ever agreeing to be your slave! I may have slept with you, but that doesn't give you any rights over my body—or my mind!'

'And I may have slept with *you*, but that doesn't give you the right to intrude into my personal life! That was a private phone call between me and my brother, and you were invading that privacy by listening! It didn't concern you.'

'Of course it didn't! After all, I'm just an unimportant little parcel that you enjoyed unwrapping at the beginning—but now that you've opened your new toy and played with it once or twice you've lost interest. I suppose the shine, the freshness has worn off and you're bored!'

'Leah, no!'

Hellfire! Whichever idiot had claimed that attack was the best form of defence wanted their head examined! They'd got it all wrong. All he had succeeded in doing was hurting her, driving her away from him.

The problem was that he was floundering in the dark, not knowing what *he* felt, let alone what was going through *her* mind. Talk about the blind leading the blind!

'It wasn't like that at all!'

Moving forward swiftly, he came to take her hand. The

stiff way she held her body away from his, the suspicion darkening her eyes tore at something deep inside him and made him tighten his grip on her fingers until she winced in pain.

'I'm sorry!'

But he wouldn't let her go. She looked like a nervous bird, poised for flight, and he was afraid she might run if he did, escape from him, and he would never get her back.

'Leah, you've got it all wrong. You only heard one side of the conversation. And it was Pete...'

'Oh, it was Pete, was it? *Pete* who said he didn't want to commit? *Pete* who didn't want me to meet his family, who thought I wasn't "the type"!'

Hearing them this way, Sean actually shuddered at the appalling sound of his own words. Why hadn't he realised how they could be interpreted? He felt as if he stood condemned by every phrase that had fallen from his lips.

'Please—it doesn't have to be like this.'

There was one way he could reach her, one way she couldn't hold out against him. Softly he trailed one hand down the side of her face, his heart clenching when he saw her stony disregard for the gentle caress.

But when he drew her nearer she came unresistingly, and she didn't turn away from the kiss he pressed onto her soft forehead, so he let a little hope slide into the haze in his mind.

'You know what you do to me, Leah. You know how I feel about you.'

His lips moved slowly down her cheek and across to her mouth. Her initial stiffness was distinctly worrying, but then with a small moan of surrender she parted her lips to the pressure of his tongue and he knew a surge of heady triumph.

'When we have this we don't need anything else, sweetheart. We shouldn't let other things get in the way...'

She was melting against him, her body soft and pliant as she swayed towards him. The loose, oversized robe proved no barrier to his urgent hands, the searching fingers that slid in at the open neck. Her skin was so soft and warm, so exciting, so inviting...

'You see...' It was a murmur of satisfaction. 'We don't have to fight. Let me take you back to bed and show you how well we can communicate. Let me—'

'No!'

Her cry echoed round the room as with a violent movement that tore at something inside him she wrenched herself from his hold, pulling the robe back across her exposed breasts and belting it tightly round her.

'I said no! I don't want this!'

'Liar! You've wanted nothing else for the past three days!'

He wished the words back as soon as he'd said them, but the damage was already done. She hadn't moved away from him physically, but mentally she was way out of his reach.

What the hell was he doing? He was driving her further away from him with every word he spoke.

'All right,' she conceded unwillingly. 'I *wanted* it, but not any more. It's not enough. Not nearly enough.'

'And what else do you want?'

He saw the change in her face, could almost read her mind, her earlier tirade playing over again inside his head.

'Commitment,' he said, his voice thickening with black cynicism. 'So that's it! The usual female trap—marriage or nothing.'

Her face was white, those amazing eyes pansy-dark above colourless cheeks.

'I never said marriage!'

But she wasn't denying that that was what she wanted either.

'But I can't just settle for nothing!'

'Nothing!' He spat the word into her face. 'Is that what these past days have been to you—*nothing*? We share a passion, a desire that's like a flame...'

'And flames burn out so quickly! I can't do it, Sean! Without love—without commitment—that passion would swallow me up, destroy me. It would be like the eclipse on Christmas Eve. The passion would be like the sun, blotting out the light of the moon—the light that is me! I wouldn't exist any more!'

As her words died away Sean drew in his breath with a ragged hiss, raking both his hands through his hair.

'Then there's no point in going on unless you can accept things as they are. Because I'm not offering permanence, Leah. I won't promise something I know I can't deliver.'

Couldn't she see that he was trying his best to be honest? Surely she could value that at least? But then even that faint hope shrivelled and died as she shook her head in firm rejection.

'And I can't live with the thought that one day—sooner rather than later—you'll tire of me and throw me out. Oh, don't try to deny it,' she hurried on as he opened his mouth to protest. 'I mean, the phone's only been back on for a couple of hours and already you've called the garage to arrange to have my car sorted out so that you can be rid of me whenever it suits.'

'It wasn't…'

But he couldn't finish. It was partially the truth, he admitted to himself, but not in the way she had interpreted it. It had been because he had wanted her to know that she was free. She could go if she wanted—or stay. But that wasn't going to happen now.

'Forget it, Sean,' Leah said softly. 'I think we both know where we stand.'

Still with her head held high, she turned and started to walk away from him.

'Where are you going now?'

'To get dressed.' It was low-voiced, flat and emotionless. 'And then perhaps you'd be kind enough to drive me to the garage.'

She was ready in no time at all. Certainly not long enough for him to collect his scattered thoughts and find a way out of the mess they were in.

There wasn't a way out. They were each on opposite

sides of a yawning chasm and nothing could build a bridge across it.

Leah collected her handbag from the living room, looking round sadly at the decorations she had made so happily such a short time before. At the last moment her gaze fell on the small, brightly wrapped parcel on the hearth.

'You never opened your present—*this* present, that is,' she amended bitterly.

'So I didn't.'

They had never even thought of it. They'd been too busy making love, too absorbed in each other to notice anything else.

'I'll leave it anyway. I certainly don't want it, and now I can't give it to—'

'You can't give it to...?' He pounced on the words viciously. 'Give it to who?'

But she didn't need to answer. Like a cold, brutal spotlight flicking on, the truth dawned in his mind.

'Andy,' he said slowly, dangerously. 'It was originally for Andy, wasn't it?'

If she'd been pale before, then now her skin was practically translucent.

'Would you believe me if I said no? And does it matter who I bought it for? I—'

'Does it matter?'

He couldn't believe how much it hurt. So much that he wanted to take her heart and tear it into little pieces in return.

'Of course it matters! Take it!' he roared, snatching it up and shoving it at her, not caring that her nerveless hands fumbled and let it drop to the floor. 'Take it and get out! Do you think I want anything like that—do you think I want his cast-offs?'

That brought her head up. Her eyes were dead and her skin drawn tight across her fine bones.

'You weren't so particular about such things when it came to sleeping with me!'

'No, I wasn't.'

Totally punch drunk on anger and pain, Sean saw his chance. Urged on by some evil little imp of cruelty, he couldn't resist the opportunity to drive the knife of revenge home and twist it hard.

'But then it's surprising how very low you'll stoop when you're desperate.'

The silence that greeted the foul words was so profound that it almost felt as if the air in the room had turned to ice. He thought he saw the glint of tears in her eyes, but she refused to let them fall as she straightened her shoulders and picked up her bag.

'How very true—for both of us, I think. Well, now we really do know where we stand.'

Drawing in a deep, uneven breath, she swallowed hard.

'Perhaps I could ask you one last favour?'

'Name it.'

Even now, he couldn't suppress the tiny, irrational hope that sprang into his mind. But it was already far too late, and her words confirmed as much when she spoke again.

'Let me use the phone to ring for a taxi. I'll wait at the garage until my car's ready. I think we'd both be a lot happier with a clean, sharp break.'

'I couldn't agree more.' He didn't know how he found the voice to say it, or the strength to make the gesture towards the study door. 'Be my guest.'

CHAPTER ELEVEN

'FIVE-FIFTEEN, thank heaven! Only a quarter of an hour to go!'

Leah smiled in sympathy as her workmate, Melanie, collapsed onto the chair in her office with an exaggerated sigh of relief.

'It's been a day from hell, hasn't it?' she said with feeling, thinking, as the younger woman nodded enthusiastic agreement, that her friend only knew the half of it.

'The world and his wife must have been in to enquire about a holiday today. It must be because of the post-Christmas slump and the appalling weather.'

She nodded towards the window, where the rain lashed against the glass.

'It makes them think longingly of warmer places, of—'

She broke off on a groan as the sound of a buzzer from the main part of the agency indicated the arrival of yet another would-be holidaymaker.

'I'll get it.'

Melanie forced herself to her feet and headed out of the room, leaving Leah to concentrate once more on the papers she had been working on.

Trying to work on, she amended wryly as she heard Melanie greet their customer. The truth was that her powers of concentration were at rock bottom, and had been from the moment she had got up. It had been like that ever since she had returned to London after the holidays, but today had been so much worse.

Sighing, she rubbed a weary hand across eyes that were dulled and shadowed with lack of sleep. A week ago she might have been able to explain away her listlessness and woolly-mindedness as the result of celebrating the New

171

Year, but that wouldn't work as a cover story for much longer.

The truth was that she had felt only half a person ever since she had left Yorkshire. She had left a vital part of herself in the cottage, with Sean. Even the happy news her mother had told her the previous night was not enough to lift the black cloud of depression.

'It's someone to see you.'

Melanie was back, standing in the doorway with her eyes wide with suppressed excitement. Seeing from Leah's face that she was about to refuse to see anyone, she went on swiftly, 'And he says he won't leave without talking to you. Says it's not business, but…'

'Strictly personal.'

The two words were pronounced in a coldly precise voice, rich with ominous undertones that had Leah freezing in the act of shaking her head. She didn't have to look up to see who now stood behind Melanie, his dark head and broad shoulders dwarfing her petite frame.

All the strength seemed to drain from her body as she looked up and found her gaze locking with those vivid blue eyes that she remembered only too well.

She had seen those eyes so many times since. They had haunted her restless, erotic dreams over the past weeks. In her sleep she had seen them glow with gentle warmth, or blaze with sexual hunger. Seen them dark with passion or glazed by desire. And then, as cruel reality had taken over, crushing her sensual imagination, she had seen them once again as cold and inimical as they were now, just shards of blue ice that seemed to freeze her right to her soul.

'Hello, Sean,' she managed, shock depriving her voice of all emotion so that it sounded cold and distantly brittle.

'Leah…'

With a curt nod of acknowledgement he put Melanie to one side and strode purposefully into the room. As he came nearer, Leah suddenly had to get to her feet in a rush, feeling far too vulnerable and defenceless sitting down.

Nervously she adjusted her smart navy skirt and white blouse.

'What can I do for you?'

It was impossible that he had simply picked on this travel agency by chance, by some dreadful malign coincidence. But at least allowing herself to think that stopped her from indulging in the crazy, weak hope that sprang into her mind.

She couldn't let herself believe that he had come looking for her alone. That he would say that he had realised how wrong he'd been, that...

Crushing down the foolish thought, she took cover behind the formally professional façade she adopted with difficult customers.

'Are you interested in a holiday? Can I help—'

The words were cut off sharply by an explicitly savage retort that had Melanie's eyes widening even further.

'You can go home now, Mel,' she said hastily. 'It's very nearly time. I'll lock up.'

'If you're sure...'

With a lingering glance at Sean that was a blend of fascination and something close to fear, the younger girl hurried from the room, and a short time late Leah heard the front door close behind her.

The sudden silence was broken by Sean's unexpected snort of cynical laughter.

'She looked as if she was torn between satisfying her curiosity as to why I was here and wanting to get the hell away from me as quickly as possible.'

I know exactly how she felt, Leah told herself silently, knowing that, with the exception of one other emotion, Sean had described the volatile mixture in her mind precisely. But that extra, unwanted feeling complicated things terribly.

It was impossible to deny the pleasure she got simply from seeing Sean here with her like this, when she had believed it would never happen again. Impossible not to let her gaze wander over the tall, strong body in a rich blue

shirt and black jeans under a supple leather flying jacket.
Impossible to resist the appeal of those strongly carved features, the black hair whipped into wild disarray by the wind
and spattered with jewel-like drops of rain.

He looked stunning, gloriously alive and virile, his devastatingly vital attraction positively lethal to her composure.

But that attraction was a double-edged sword. It slashed
though the control she had thought she had imposed on
herself ever since she had fled from the cottage and returned
home. For the delight of seeing him, speaking to him like
this, she knew she would have to pay a hundredfold. It
would mean enduring the agony of loss all over again, the
sleepless nights and the long, lonely days.

'Just why *have* you come here?'

But she was talking to empty air. Sean had turned on his
heel and marched out of the room. Following him help-
lessly, Leah could only stare in confusion as he fastened
the lock and slammed home the bolts on the door through
which Melanie had just left, pulling down the blinds at the
windows.

'Sean! It's not closing time…'

'Near enough,' he declared, coming back towards her,
switching off lights as he went. 'After all, there are hardly
great queues of people banging on the door demanding to
be let in. Anyone with any sense will be on their way home
to get out of this rain and stay indoors for the rest of the
night. Get your coat.'

But Leah had decided that the time had come to dig in
her heels and assert herself. Up to now she'd felt as if she
had been flattened by a tidal wave, but enough was enough.

'Not on your life!' she retorted, her chin coming up defiantly. 'I'm not going anywhere with you for any reason
at all!'

'We need to talk.' The harsh assertion slashed through
her protest.

'About what?'

Oh, why was she still a prey to that weak flare of hope
that ran like lightning through every nerve, setting her on

fire with yearning hunger? In the end, it only made the inevitable let-down all the worse when Sean reached into his coat pocket and pulled out a folded newspaper, tossing it onto the desk beside her.

There was no need to ask any further what he meant. The paper fell open at the appropriate page, its message clear for her to see.

Leah had to bite back a moan of despair as her eyes focused on the photograph of Sean's face, the scarred side showing shockingly clearly, underneath the dark, mocking headline: WHO'S NOT A PRETTY BOY, THEN?

Stunned into silence, the power of speech totally deserting her, Leah could only open and close her mouth again without a sound coming out.

'*Coat!*' Sean instructed again, with deadly intensity.

Moving purely on automatic pilot, she obeyed, checking doors and setting the alarm like a programmed robot. He couldn't suspect... He just *couldn't* believe she was capable...

It wasn't until he had led her to his car, installed her in the front seat and was actually driving away that rational thought returned, and with it some control over her voice.

'Where are you taking me?' It was impossible not to remember how she had been through something very like this before, and the recollection of what that had led to sent a cold shiver down her spine.

'Somewhere we can talk undisturbed.'

'But you can't think I...'

For a second his eyes left the road and fixed her with an intent scrutiny that made her feel as if she might actually shrivel into ashes in her seat.

'Who else is there?'

Who else, indeed? It was a consideration that kept her silent again until he swung the car into an underground car park, slamming on the brakes before getting out to open her door.

Terror held her frozen in her seat. Looking into the inimical blue of his eyes, she could almost hear again his

voice saying harshly, 'It would make a great exclusive…
Everyone could do with a little bit more money.'

'Sean, be reasonable. How could I have done this? I
didn't even have a camera. And I wouldn't tell anyone…'
The words tumbled over each other in her rush to try and
convince him. 'I mean, I *couldn't*! You know I wouldn't
because—'

Realisation of exactly what she had been about to give
away closed her throat over the words 'I love you'. Sean
ignored her appeal, his face set in cold, unyielding lines.

'Are you coming, or do I have to…?'

Abruptly his mood changed. Drawing a deep, ragged
breath, he raked both hands through the dark sleekness of
his hair.

'Leah…' he began again, in a very different voice, the
contrast with his previous tone almost shocking. 'Please
come with me to my flat, so that we can talk like civilised
human beings.'

'"Civilised"!' Leah scoffed. 'There's been very little
that was *civil* about the way you've behaved up till now!'
But that unexpected note of appeal had her climbing out of
the car when all the force in the world wouldn't have
moved her.

In the lift up to his flat they remained silent, Sean appearing to have lapsed into a dark and brooding mood, his
thoughts obviously ones that disturbed him.

After the stark simplicity of the cottage, the muted luxury
of the room he led her into took her breath away. Decorated
in tones of beige and cream, with lots of natural pale wood,
it was a painful reminder of the fact that the man who lived
there was the real Sean Gallagher, rich, famous, and very,
very successful. The brief idyll of the Yorkshire hideaway
had never seemed more dreamlike and unreal.

'Would you like a drink?'

Automatically Leah shook her head. She knew she
couldn't blame the effects of alcohol for what had happened
the last time they had been together, but all the same she
thought it was wiser to keep a very clear head. As he

poured himself a measure of brandy, she launched into an appeal for understanding.

'Sean, you must know that I would never have sold your story to the papers. It's something that's a total anathema to me.'

He took a large swallow of his drink, watching her closely over the rim of his glass.

'And you expect me to believe that?'

'Why not? It is the truth after all.'

'Is it?'

'Of course it is! If you must know, I don't even *see* that scar any more, or only because it's part of you—like your hair or your eyes—and if the television people think—'

'They don't,' Sean inserted firmly. 'The producers of *Inspector Callender* don't give a damn about the scar. As a matter of fact, they've come up with a major storyline to explain how it happened—one I'm really looking forward to acting.'

'I'm glad…'

'And I may no longer be ''God's gift to women''….' The cynical way he quoted her own description back at her again made Leah wince in distress. 'But in a way that's all to the good. There are plenty of meaty parts for someone who's no longer tied to the matinée idol label. So if you thought that making the story a nine-day wonder would—'

'I *didn't*!' How could she make him believe her? 'The time I spent with you in the cottage isn't something I'd want to share with anyone else, let alone the papers.'

'And why not?'

Because I love you! But she couldn't say that, not when he was glowering at her in that threatening manner, his dark, straight brows drawn tightly together.

'Because I—care about you.'

'*Care!*' It was like a crack of thunder, cynical enough to make her flinch. 'Oh, yes, you care, all right. Enough to take what you want while you're enjoying yourself, but not enough to stick around when things get tough.'

'No!'

How could he accuse her of that? Hadn't he been the
one to force her out? Or was he saying that if she'd stayed,
pushed—tried a little harder...?

'No?'

His sudden movement towards her had her whirling
away in panic, sending her bag flying so that it landed on
the floor. The impact snapped open the clasp, sending the
contents tumbling onto the carpet. With a cry of distress
she knelt to gather them up again.

'Here, let me...'

He was at her side in a moment. Together their hands
reached for the same item—a square white envelope.
Sean's fingers closed over it first.

'Give that to me!'

Her panic-stricken reaction was a mistake, alerting him
to its importance. Leah's heart clenched painfully as she
saw his considering frown, watched him turn it over to see
the address on the front. His address.

'What's this?'

'A birthday card.' There was little point in denying it
now. 'I—happy birthday for today, Sean.'

Something crossed his face, some emotion she could not
fully understand. It was raw and harsh and shockingly unconcealed.

'But you didn't send it.'

'I had second thoughts.' And third, and fourth. 'I thought
perhaps it was wiser not to...'

'Wiser.' Those blue eyes wouldn't meet hers, but stared
down at his own name printed on the envelope. 'But you
thought about writing to me. Why?'

Suddenly he got to his feet in a swift, lithe movement,
his hand taking hers, pulling her up with him.

'Are you all right, Leah?' The question was sharp, urgent, seemingly out of all proportion to the very minor accident of a moment before.

'Yes, of course...'

'Believe me, I'm not usually so irresponsible, but that
first time...'

It was then that the reality of what he meant dawned on her. 'All right' meant all right *physically*. In the cottage, he had insisted on taking responsibility for birth control, but in the first rush of overwhelming passion neither of them had stopped to think.

'There's no baby, if that's what you mean.'

Of course he wouldn't want any repercussions, anything that would give the scandal rags something to write about.

'Have you spoken to Andy?'

'Yes.' She couldn't manage any more, totally bewildered by the apparent *non sequitur*.

'You told him you couldn't marry him?' At her silent nod he continued softly, 'Was it very difficult?'

'Very.' The suddenly sympathetic intonation was so unexpected that she could do nothing but answer him straight. 'I didn't enjoy it, if that's what you mean! But I knew I could never have made him happy.'

'And what about you?'

'I would never have been happy with him.'

How could she be when the only man she loved, the one person who could make her happy for the rest of her life, was standing right beside her, his face wearing the same darkly brooding look that she had seen on it in the lift?

'And you're sure you're not pregnant?'

'Positive! You needn't worry. There won't be any "TV Hunk Fathered my Lovechild in Hideaway Love-Nest" headlines.'

Deliberately she mocked his own words. Was it really no more than a few weeks since he had spoken them? She felt as if she had lived through a thousand lifetimes since then.

What was there in those dark eyes? What had drawn his skin so tightly over the bones of his face? She couldn't begin to guess, and his response was so unexpected that her thought processes stopped dead.

'Pity,' he murmured, or at least that was what she thought she'd heard.

'Did you say...?'

'I said it's a pity you're not pregnant,' Sean declared, so clearly that there was no possibility of misunderstanding.

'But *why?*'

A faint, rueful smile touched the corners of his mouth for a second, and then vanished again.

'Because if you were then at least I'd have a chance of persuading you to marry me.'

'To *marry*...Sean, you're not making any sense. What do you mean...?'

This time the smile was stronger, but worryingly sardonic.

'What does it usually mean when a man wants a woman to marry him? It means he loves her more than life itself, that he wants to be with her for ever...'

'But you don't believe in love for ever!'

'I didn't.'

Suddenly all trace of aggression had dropped away, and in its place was an open vulnerability that tugged sharply at Leah's heart. She had never seen Sean like this before, with all his defences down, no restraint, no concealment.

He was still holding her hand too, she realised, his fingers curled round it softly but firmly.

'I thought the idea of loving one person for the rest of your days was just a myth—pure fantasy. But then you came into my life and turned it upside down, and suddenly I didn't know what to think about anything any more.'

'But you threw me out.'

The look in those deep blue eyes seared over her skin, stilling her tongue when she would have said more.

'I was *scared*—frightened of what was happening to me! I didn't recognise myself in what I was doing, the way I was thinking. I was afraid to open up to it, to accept the commitment it asked for—you asked for.'

'I couldn't accept anything less.'

Leah's grip tightened on his hand as she willed him to understand.

'You know I want a marriage like the one my parents have. I believed I could love Andy, but then, having met you, it was as if an atom bomb had exploded in my face. I knew then that there was no one else in the world for me, that I would love you for ever, and I wanted you with me for the rest of my life. If I couldn't have that, then nothing else would do.'

'Leah...' Sean began, but she couldn't let him stop her. She had to let him know the whole truth, no half-measures. She couldn't bear it if he believed that she had casually exchanged one so-called love for another.

'The contrast between those two very different ways of caring showed me what *loving* really meant, and I knew that if you didn't feel the same about me then I couldn't stay, no matter how much I wanted to. I just couldn't take second best, couldn't stay and watch what you did feel shrivel and die—as it must, without commitment, but as it would never do for me.'

'But it would never shrivel and die,' Sean put in. He laid his fingers over her mouth when she would have spoken. 'Hush, let me explain.'

For a long drawn-out moment he was silent, midnight eyes fixed on her face. Then he drew in a long, deep breath and let it out again in a heavy sigh.

'I didn't believe in love for ever, in promising to stay with one person for ever, because experience had taught me that it wasn't realistic. And I didn't think that I could ever feel enough for someone even to want to try. But when you left I was forced to realise that every day without you was an eternity. I couldn't eat, couldn't sleep. My only thoughts were of you—missing you. I dreamed of you at night and woke up aching, lonely and empty.'

'I know! Believe me, I know.' All the long, miserable days since she had seen him put the emotion into Leah's voice. 'What happened to change things?'

'My brother's wedding.'

At her start of frank surprise his smile grew again, but this time there was a new and gentler warmth in it that soothed the ache in Leah's heart, lifted her spirits.

'Yes, Pete finally married his errant fiancée. The ceremony was yesterday...'

He slanted a questioning glance at her face.

'You weren't there?'

'No—I—pressure of work.' She couldn't bring herself to admit that she'd chickened out. That, knowing he must be there, she hadn't been able to face the prospect of seeing him again.

'I missed you. And as soon as it was over I drove like a bat out of hell down to London to find you.'

'But why?'

'Why? I suddenly realised I hadn't been thinking straight. I was Pete's best man, and as I stood beside him and heard him promise to love Annie until death parted them I saw his face—and hers—and the light in their eyes, the happiness they shared. And then I thought of the prospect of dying without ever having seen you again.'

The convulsive shudder he gave was a more eloquent testimony to his feelings than any words could ever be.

'I knew I didn't want to live without you, but that commitment seemed so huge.'

'It is.' Leah's voice was low. 'I'll admit that I was quite terrified by the enormity of it—that I was afraid of the full significance of what I felt.'

She saw the flare of response deep in his eyes and knew how much the honesty of her admission meant to him.

'But you had more courage than I did. You were able to say what you felt. Even Pete, my kid brother, was braver than me.'

'He hadn't felt the loss of your father, as you had. And he hadn't known Marnie and...'

'Shh!'

Once more Sean laid his fingers over her mouth to silence her.

'Don't talk about them; they're all in the past. I want to make the future so very different. Do you think we can manage that?'

Some tiny trace of uncertainty must still have shown in

her eyes, because he suddenly led her to a chair and eased her down into it, sitting on the arm beside her.

'Let me finish—tell you everything. I'd come so far and yet not quite far enough. But then my foolish brain finally put it into words even I could understand. I realised that for ever is just a series of days—one after the other, but taken one at a time. And I wanted to spend all of those days with you.'

'And *I* want to spend them with you,' Leah put in softly, earning herself a deep, lingering kiss that threatened to put an end to any further explanations. But at last Sean lifted his head with a sigh, cradling her against his shoulder as he went on.

'I couldn't bear the thought of another twenty-four hours without you, and so I came to London and started working my way through every damn travel agency in Wimbledon. That photograph was just an excuse. Deep down, I knew that you'd had nothing to do with it, but I felt I needed something to give me a reason for looking for you in case you really didn't want to see me.'

'I'd never have been able to say no to you,' Leah told him honestly. 'I would have had to see you just once more. Did you really try *every* agency?'

'Why do you think I didn't find you until almost half past five? Can you even begin to guess just how many travel agents there are round here? And if I hadn't found you today, I'd have started again tomorrow.'

'I'm glad my agency was on today's itinerary,' Leah said, heartfelt relief sounding in her voice. 'I don't think I could have borne to be without you for another night.'

Looking up into Sean's face, she caught his sudden thoughtful frown.

'What is it?'

He was obviously reviewing their conversation, thinking back over all that had been said.

'You said "the sort of marriage that your parents *have*"?'

'That's right.'

Her smile lit up her whole face, her eyes glowing like
polished amethysts.

'It's all sorted out. Dad's gone back to Mum and they're
happier than ever. He says that it must have been some sort
of mid-life crisis, that as soon as he'd left he knew it was
the worst mistake of his life, but his pride got in the way
and wouldn't let him admit it.'

'Men!' Sean shook his head at the behaviour of his own
sex. 'We're pretty thick sometimes when it comes to ex-
pressing our feelings. What gave him the push in the end?'

'You did, in a way. When you rang up and told Mum I
was with you, she used it as an excuse to ring Dad.'

'She was worried?' Sean asked, and saw her smile grow,
become mischievous.

'She can't have been,' she said, laughter bubbling up
under her words. 'Because she told Dad she was convinced
she'd just been talking to the man who was going to become their son-in-law.'

'She knew! But how?'

'Something in your voice, she said. The way you spoke
my name.'

The glint of amusement in those blue eyes matched her
own as Sean shook his head again, this time in bewilderment.

'So I was hooked, even then? Even my prospective
mother-in-law saw it before I did myself.'

'Mother's intuition,' Leah assured him. 'She's famous
for it.'

'Well, I couldn't be happier that they're back together.
That way, your father will be able to give you away when
you marry me.'

When, Leah noted, not if. This man of hers had taken a
while to come round to the idea of commitment, but once
he had his undertaking was deep and total, a promise for
life, with no prospect of second thoughts.

Getting to her feet, she linked her arms around his neck
and looked deep into his loving eyes.

'My father will walk me down the aisle, Sean,' she told

him softly. 'But he won't be giving me away. You see, *I* did that from the first moment that I met you. I gave my heart away to you then, and I never, ever want it back.'

'I'll keep it safe.' Sean's reply was a huskily intent whisper. 'Just as you must keep mine, for today and tomorrow, and all the tomorrows after. I'm going to use all the hours I have to show you just what you mean to me, and how much I adore you—starting right now!'

And as he swung her up into his arms, carrying her towards the stairs and his bedroom, Leah knew that the passion they shared would never eclipse their love, as she had feared. Instead, now that it was combined with honesty and commitment that would deepen and enhance it, that passion could only burn even brighter for the rest of their lives.

Tyler Brides

It happened one weekend...

Quinn and Molly Spencer are delighted to accept three bookings for their newly opened B&B, Breakfast Inn Bed, located in America's favorite hometown, Tyler, Wisconsin.

But Gina Santori is anything but thrilled to discover her best friend has tricked her into sharing a room with the man who broke her heart eight years ago....

And Delia Mayhew can hardly believe that she's gotten herself locked in the Breakfast Inn Bed basement with the sexiest man in America.

Then there's Rebecca Salter. She's turned up at the Inn in her wedding gown. Minus her groom.

Come home to Tyler for three delightful novellas by three of your favorite authors: Kristine Rolofson, Heather MacAllister and Jacqueline Diamond.

HARLEQUIN®
Makes any time special ™

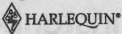

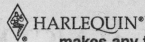